Twelve military heroes.
Twelve indomitable heroines.
One UNIFORMLY HOT! miniseries.

Don't miss Harlequin Blaze's first 12-book continuity series, featuring irresistible soldiers from all branches of the armed forces.

Watch for:

LETTERS FROM HOME by Rhonda Nelson
(Army Rangers—June 2009)

THE SOLDIER by Rhonda Nelson
(Special Forces—July 2009)

STORM WATCH by Jill Shalvis
(National Guard—August 2009)

HER LAST LINE OF DEFENSE by Marie Donovan
(Green Berets—September 2009)

RIPPED! by Jennifer LaBrecque
(Paratrooper—October 2009)

SEALED AND DELIVERED by Jill Monroe
(Navy SEALs—November 2009)

CHRISTMAS MALE by Cara Summers
(Military Police—December 2009)

Uniformly Hot!
The Few. The Proud. The Sexy as Hell.

Dear Reader,

When I wrote three connected firefighter books last summer (*Flashpoint, Flashback* and *Heating Up the Holidays*), I had a niggling feeling I wasn't ready to be finished with these guys. So I gave my hero in *Heating Up the Holidays* a brother—a military guy, dark and edgy and just a little bit tortured—just in case.

Thankfully my editor had the same thought. So I'd like to introduce you to Jason. He's home after giving eight years to good old Uncle Sam, and he's not sure how he feels about that. Should he reenlist? Stick with his hometown and try to reconnect? He just doesn't know, and after losing his best friend in a rescue operation, he's not sure he even cares.

Until he runs into a blast from his past. Lizzy. The girl who'd once haunted him with nothing but her pretty eyes. She's all grown up now. Grown up and developed a bit of a 'tude. But hey, since he's got one himself, he can appreciate that. Pitching these two against each other was great fun. I'm only sorry it's over.

Happy reading! I'll see you next summer when I revisit Santa Rey. Only this time I've got a few sexy cops lined up to heat up your nights.

Enjoy,

Jill Shalvis

Jill Shalvis

STORM WATCH

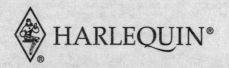

TORONTO • NEW YORK • LONDON
AMSTERDAM • PARIS • SYDNEY • HAMBURG
STOCKHOLM • ATHENS • TOKYO • MILAN • MADRID
PRAGUE • WARSAW • BUDAPEST • AUCKLAND

Recycling programs
for this product may
not exist in your area.

ISBN-13: 978-0-373-79491-1

STORM WATCH

Copyright © 2009 by Jill Shalvis.

This edition published by arrangement with Harlequin Books S.A.

® and TM are trademarks of the publisher. Trademarks indicated with
® are registered in the United States Patent and Trademark Office, the
Canadian Trade Marks Office and in other countries.

www.eHarlequin.com

Printed in U.S.A.

ABOUT THE AUTHOR

USA TODAY bestselling author Jill Shalvis is happily writing her next book from her neck of the Sierras. You can find her books wherever romance novels are sold, or visit her on the Web at www.jillshalvis.com.

Books by Jill Shalvis

Don't miss any of our special offers. Write to us at the following address for information on our newest releases.

Harlequin Reader Service
U.S.: 3010 Walden Ave., P.O. Box 1325, Buffalo, NY 14269
Canadian: P.O. Box 609, Fort Erie, Ont. L2A 5X3

To Brenda Chin, for letting me write all these sexy firefighters and military heroes my way. Okay, it's your way, but you let me think it's my way. The mark of a great editor...

1

JASON MAUER STAGGERED through the fifty-mile-an-hour winds and into the house with three things on his mind—food, sleep and sex.

Thanks to Uncle Sam and the National Guard, he hadn't been home for any real length of time in years, home being the small California beach town of Santa Rey. When he was in town, he shared a house with his brother, Dustin, and hoped to find the fridge stocked with at least sandwich makings and, please God, a beer or two.

As for the sleep...well, he had a bedroom. The question was could he shut down enough, push away the haunting memories long enough to actually get some shut-eye.

The jury was still out on that one.

Which left sex.

He needed a woman for that, at least the way he liked it, and seeing as he'd been working his ass off on his last military stint, spending some special quality time at every national disaster that had hit the news, plus a bunch that hadn't, he was fairly certain he was lucky just to be alive, much less naked with a woman.

With a bone-weary sigh, he dropped his gear and headed directly toward the refrigerator. He should call his brother, his sister and his mom, and let them know he was back a few days early…but they'd be all over him, wondering if he was really okay, if he'd recovered from his loss.

He hadn't.

So he didn't call, not yet. Instead, he looked out the windows into the growing dark, even though it was barely five o'clock in the afternoon in June. From the kitchen window, he watched the ocean pound the shore, the waves pushing fifteen feet minimum. The winds had stirred up some seriously ominous clouds, and he was surprised to see trees doubled over from the gusts.

He'd seen bad weather in his time—hello, hurricanes Rita and Katrina—but nothing here on the supposedly mild Central California coast.

His stomach growled, reminding him that it'd taken him all day and three flights to get here, bad storm or not, and he couldn't remember the last thing he'd eaten. Peanuts, given to him by a cute flight attendant? No, a candy bar grabbed at the airport.

And the damn fridge was empty.

Yeah. Pretty much how his life felt at the moment. Empty as hell. Matt would laugh at that and tell him to get over himself.

But Matt was dead, six weeks now.

Still shell-shocked, Jason's gut clenched hard at the thought of his best friend lying six feet under, and suddenly he was no longer hungry. Fuck it, he thought. Fuck thinking, he was going directly to bed, no passing Go. He kicked off his shoes, and so damn tired he practically staggered like a drunk, moved down the hallway. He was "in the tween" as his sister, Shelly, would say. In between military life, which was all he'd known since high school, and his old life, which no longer even seemed real.

Which world did he want?

The government wanted him back, of course. He was highly trained and valuable. That wasn't ego, but fact. He was a rescue expert who worked with nerves of steel. Or he had…

His family was hoping he'd stick here. His mother, living twenty miles north of Santa Rey in San Luis Obispo, wanted him to be safe and sound. His sister, who lived with her while going to Cal Poly, wanted him to date her friends. Dustin—here in Santa Rey—was his partner in their on-the-side renovation business, and wanted him home to be a more active presence.

As for what Jason wanted? No clue. None. Zero. Zip.

But he had a few weeks to figure it out. With a sigh, he looked around the empty house. Dustin lived with his fiancé, Cristina, most of the time these days, which left the place looking a bit neglected. It'd been

just waiting for him to come back to help Dustin finish the upgrades, so they could sell it and move on to
the next project. Dustin had redone the kitchen and
both bathrooms. He'd pulled the carpet and refin-
ished the original hardwood floors. And he'd done a
good job, too. All that was left was a couple coats of
paint and some tile in the entry, and this house could
be flipped, something Dustin was eager to do.

As for himself, he was having a hard time caring.
About anything—except his three simple needs.

Since there was no food and no willing woman,
he'd get right to the sleeping portion of the evening.
The room was furnished—as opposed to the last time
he'd seen it, when it'd just had a mattress on the un-
finished floor. Now there was oversize knotty pine
furniture, complete with a king-size bed. It seemed
hugely luxurious compared to what he was used to,
and it hit him.

He really was back in the real world.

Physically, anyway. Mentally? Not yet. Not even
close. He didn't even know if he could come back to
his world and not be ready to protect and serve
twenty-four/seven. Not be hard and cold and willing
to do whatever it took...

Be normal.

With the wind continuing to batter the house, he
stripped off his shirt and flicked on the small TV
over the dresser.

No reception.

He pulled out his cell phone and searched for the weather, and discovered the reason. Apparently he'd walked into an unprecedented storm, with even heavier rain and wind expected. For an extra bonus, flash-floods warnings were in effect.

Wasn't that special. He hadn't dealt with a flood since six weeks ago, in the Midwest, where his unit had been called in to assist with SAR.

He and Matt had both gone in, but only Jason had come out.

Yeah. This was going to be a kick.

He headed straight for the bed and felt some of the tension leave him in anticipation of sleep. With a long sigh, he stripped out of his pants, then stretched out on the mattress with only his boxer briefs and dark thoughts.

Tired and edgy, and feeling old for his twenty-nine years, he let himself relax, hoping like hell he was too far gone into exhaustion to dream. As he drifted off to the wild winds pummeling the house, his stomach growled, and he promised it that even if a naked woman appeared at his side right then and there, *food*—not sex—was next on the list.

JASON AWOKE with a jerk and leaped to his feet to run for his gear. When he realized he wasn't on the line but back at home, he lay down again and swiped a hand over his face as the rain and wind continued to batter the house around him.

He didn't like to admit that he wasn't decompressing fast enough, or that his hand was trembling, but he'd deal with both. Because that's what he did—deal with things. That was his claim to fame, his skill, his MO.

Letting out another long, careful breath, he took in his surroundings and realized it was nearly dawn.

Which meant he'd slept straight through the night.

And then he realized something else. He'd been awoken by an assortment of brain-racking noises. The crazy wind. The steady drum of rain pounding on the roof and the windows.

Adding to the racket was the ringing of a phone, and then the click of a message machine.

"You know what to do at the beep," came Dustin's recorded voice from somewhere nearby.

And then a soft, female voice, crackling through static and hard to hear. "Dustin? Dustin, are you there?"

The male in Jason, the one who hadn't been with a woman in so long, took in the pretty voice and thought, *Go, Dustin,* but even through the incredibly bad connection, he recognized that she wasn't trying to be seductive and fun. No, she was filled with nerves. Something within Jason automatically reacted to that, the same something that had put him in the military in the first place, the thing that made it impossible for him to walk away from a fight or someone in trouble, and he lifted his head, searching the still dark room for the phone.

There wasn't one, not in here.

"I think I need help," she went on as Jason ran out of the bedroom to find the phone, wondering if she was Cristina, Dustin's fiancé. With the horrible connection, there was no way to tell for sure, but he doubted it. The Cristina he knew didn't ask for help.

He finally narrowed in on a blinking red light on the nightstand in Dustin's bedroom, and knew he'd found the machine. He reached for the phone connected to it, but the receiver wasn't in its cradle. *"Shit."*

"Dustin?" she said again, her voice breaking up with static.

Jason could hear the storm ravaging in the background, both through the phone and the windows, coming in with unexpected surround sound.

"I know you're not scheduled to work this weekend," she went on, "so I'm really hoping you're there."

"Hang on," Jason told the machine and slapped on the light, squinting into the sudden brightness as he searched for the on-the-loose phone. *Gotcha*, he thought triumphantly, eyeing the cordless handset lying on a dresser. He hit the talk button with his thumb and…nothing.

The battery was dead.

"Don't hang up," he yelled at the machine as if she could hear him, and once again went running, slamming his shoulder into the doorway. "Goddammit." In the living room, he looked around in the wan light for another phone.

There. On the small table beside the couch. Lunging for it, he barked *"Hello!"* into the receiver, just in time to hear the click.

He'd lost her.

He was getting good at that, losing people—and yeah, there it was, right on cue, the helplessness surging up into his chest, making it impossible to breathe without pain.

He rounded back toward the bedroom, holding his aching shoulder, going for his cell phone. Seemed he was on a mission after all—to first find Dustin and then, through him, hopefully the woman with the worry in her voice, the woman who needed help.

As LIZZY MANN TOSSED aside her cell phone and drove through winds that were jarring her little Honda around like it was nothing more than a Matchbox car, she wished her sister would call again. Not that wishing had ever gotten her anywhere with Cece.

Ever.

"Evacuations are beginning," the deejay announced through her radio, and Lizzy tensed.

"The Santa Rey bowl is filling up, starting at Main," he said. "All the way to the high school."

"Don't say Eastside," she murmured, glancing at the radio as if she could actually affect the report. "Please. Please, don't say—"

"And all of Eastside, starting at Second."

Naturally, and for Lizzy, the storm took a right turn

from nasty into Hell-ville. Because Eastside was where she had to go. *Of course* it was where she had to go. Because this wouldn't be a Cece situation if it didn't put Lizzy in danger or jeopardy.

Not fair, Lizzy reminded herself. Her sister had changed. She really had. Yes, growing up after losing their parents meant that Lizzy had always been the mom, the one in charge, but now they were *both* adults. And what might have started out as a New Year's resolution, a slightly drunken one, had become a new life's resolve for Cece. Her baby sister was getting her stuff together, turning things around. No more drinking, drugs, lying and, especially, no more wild men. No more men period.

Actually, they'd *both* made that vow.

Since then, for the past six months, Lizzy had watched Cece bloom into a determined, independent twenty-four-year-old, which had been amazing to witness.

But that was about to be tested, because her sister was alone in this storm, and given her lifelong fear of them, she was also most likely terrified. And an alone, terrified Cece was never a good thing.

Sure, they'd talked earlier, at Lizzy's midnight break at the hospital, where she worked as an E.R. nurse. Cece had sworn she was fine. But now she wasn't answering her phone.

Lizzy was well aware that this was all her hang-up, that Cece was smart enough to evacuate, but

Lizzy had been the mom for so long she couldn't rest until she knew for certain.

Especially now that Cece was pregnant…

Unfortunately Lizzy's car wasn't equipped for driving in these conditions. Her tires were shot, and with the roads under a few inches of water, there was no way she could get to Third Avenue, where Cece had moved shortly after her transformation six months ago.

She'd called her neighbor, an ex-cop named Mike, but he hadn't picked up. She'd left him a message to keep an eye on her place, and let her know if anyone showed up there. Her next call had been to Dustin. They were friends from the hospital where Dustin, an EMT, often delivered patients. She had a whole group of friends from the hospital who would have helped, but for proximity reasons, she'd tagged Dustin as her best bet. He could get to Third in the storm with his SUV. All she had to do was find him. She knew he wasn't scheduled to work at the firehouse today, and he wasn't at Cristina's place—she'd checked.

Which meant he had to be home. Hopefully.

"Going to get more than twenty-four inches of rain," the deejay said. *"Crazy."*

Two feet of rain, Lizzy thought, her fingers tightening on the steering wheel. Two feet in *California*. It boggled her mind. On a good day, Santa Rey was a sweet, little, quirky, fun beach town, with tourists filling the unique downtown streets, enjoying the outdoor cafés, shops and art galleries while skateboarders and old ladies alike vied for the wide oak-lined sidewalks.

Not today.

Today, Lizzy was alone on the roads, the beach void of the surfers and tan seekers.

She turned onto Dustin's street, water spraying up on her windshield from the already flooded curbs, blinding her for a second. The only car in his driveway was a Jeep she didn't recognize, but Dustin had a huge garage. If he was home, and she hoped like hell that he was, he'd be parked inside. Pulling up the hood on her thin hoodie sweatshirt, she opened her car door.

And stepped into several inches of water.

The icy wetness seeped up into the hospital scrubs she hadn't taken the time to change out of, the thin cotton clinging to her calves and sucking the breath out of her lungs. She eyed Dustin's house, which, like her own, was on a raised foundation, as were most of the other houses on this street, and therefore elevated off the ground. Hopefully, the concrete footings would be enough to keep them from flooding.

Unfortunately, Santa Rey sat squarely between a set of low, gently rolling hills on the east and the Pacific Ocean on the west, in a little nature-made bowl of a valley.

Now with fifteen-foot swells threatening to rise even higher, and the heavy rainfall steadily sliding down the mountains with no growth to stop it thanks to last year's tragic wildfires, that bowl was filling up.

Leaving the town in serious trouble.

By profession, Lizzy was good in an emergency. Her job depended on it. She was strong of mind and body and spirit, and she knew how to be cool, calm and collected.

Or at least appear that way.

But right now, she was having a hard time. She just needed to see Cece, and then she'd relax.

Sloshing through the water up Dustin's front path, the driving wind nearly knocked her off her feet. At the door, she pounded her fist on the wood to be heard over the unbelievable din of the storm raging around her, and reached for the doorknob at the same time, surprised and relieved when it turned in her fingers. "Hello!" she called out into the dark house. "Dustin? It's me…"

The living room and kitchen lights weren't on, but she saw a light coming from down the hall. She turned back and fought the front door closed. "Dustin? Cristina?"

In answer, a shadow came along the hall. A very tall, built shadow, over six feet. But here was the thing—Dustin wasn't six feet. Plus he had a long, lanky runner's body that tended toward skinny.

Truth was, Dustin looked like Harry Potter all grown-up, complete with the sweet and kind characteristics—*not* like his body had been honed into a lean, mean, fighting machine.

Such as the one heading toward her.

Uh-oh.

He kept coming at her, in tune to the house shuddering and moaning around them, like something out of a horror movie, and she reminded herself that horror movies made her laugh. But she instinctively moved back a step, tripping over her own two very wet feet and—

Landed on her ass.

She'd been doing Tae Bo for at least five years. She should be able to kung fu his ass—all she had to do was stand up and execute a roundhouse kick—

Except the shadow crouched down to her level. "Are you okay?"

The question only further scattered her brain. Why would a bad guy ask her if she was okay? "Keep your mitts off me."

"Okay." He lifted them in surrender. "Are you the woman who called here? Do you need help?"

Dawn had barely broken and, with no lights, he was still nothing more than a dark outline of a man. A very tall, built man that she blinked up at. "How did you know I called?"

"Because I was trying to get to the phone. I couldn't find it, and then when I did, the battery was dead."

He didn't sound like a bad guy. He sounded like a sleepy, slightly irritated guy who'd been woken up, his voice low and raspy.

"You hung up too fast," he told her.

Yeah, definitely irritated.

And also, oddly familiar. *Who the hell was he?*

2

"CAN YOU HEAR ME?" he asked her. "Are you okay?"

Lizzy knew that voice. How did she know that voice?

Why did she know that voice?

The guy straightened to his full height. She heard a click, and then the room was filled with light from a lamp next to the couch.

Her bad guy was wearing a pair of army-green boxer briefs.

And nothing else.

Well, except a gorgeous body that appeared to have been chiseled with the same care and build of a Greek god, layered with sinew and sleek, tanned skin and dipped in testosterone for good measure.

Holy smokes. "Um." She shoved back her hood. "I'm looking for Dustin—" But as she focused in on him, specifically on the tribal band tattoo on his biceps, she broke off her words. He had a tat on his pec, too, a military troop number, which was new, but the one on his arm was not, and her gaze jerked up to his face.

His voice had been familiar for a reason, and her

confusion vanished, replaced by shock and surprise, and not a happy one at that. Yeah, she knew him—as the bane of her existence.

At least that's who he'd been in high school— Jason Mauer.

Dustin's brother.

He was staring at her, as well, full recognition on his face. "Wow. Lizzy Mann, all grown up."

"I was about to say the same."

At her bring-on-the-icicles tone, his lips curved. "So you're still uptight and pissy, I see."

"I have my moments. You still an ass?"

He laughed, the sound low and rusty, as if maybe he hadn't laughed in a long time. "Have my moments." He eyed her scrubs. "Dr. Mann now, right?"

Everyone in Santa Rey had known she'd gotten a full ride scholarship to UCLA to follow her childhood dream of becoming a doctor. Apparently he didn't know that she hadn't actually gone, that she'd stayed here and raised Cece, and was only now pursuing that dream again, thanks to a grant her hospital had just awarded her to go to medical school in the fall. "No. Just Lizzy. What are you doing here? I thought you were in the National Guard."

"I am. Was."

"You're out?"

He spread his hands and lifted his shoulders, as if not sure. "In between gigs, I guess you could say."

Because their last names had both started with M,

she'd sat next to him in every single class from elementary school all the way through to graduation. She hadn't talked much—she hadn't been able to, what with tripping over her tongue every time she so much as looked at him.

Which hadn't mattered because he hadn't looked at her in return. He'd been far too busy being both a football and a basketball star. Oh, and being popular. And going after every girl in school—except her.

Yeah, when it came to Jason, her teenage memories were all some variety of the same theme— humiliation and resignation. That wouldn't be the case for him. He'd been a restless student, far more into his sports than his studies, but it hadn't mattered. Not with his easygoing, laid-back charm. The teachers had fallen all over him, always making Lizzy help him catch up when he missed school for a game. That she'd been so shy as to make that nearly impossible had amused him to no end. He'd spent endless hours entertaining himself at her expense, either making her repeat a lengthy explanation just to watch her trip over her tongue, or playing dumb until she'd lose her patience with him.

And then he'd lean back with all that athletic grace and gorgeousness, all stretched out and lazy as hell, and grin.

She'd hated him.

And she'd loved him.

Horrifying and simple as that.

It'd ended when they'd graduated. He'd left immediately for the National Guard, and she'd gone off to
UCLA—except she hadn't. Nope, her dreams had
been sidelined when her parents had gotten themselves killed flying over the Grand Canyon in a stunt
plane—their anniversary gift to each other.

And she'd given up her scholarships and stayed in
town to raise her thirteen-year-old sister.

"So, talk about a blast from the past, huh?" he
asked in that low, sort of gravelly voice that used to
make her squirm in her seat.

Yes, but since that past, she'd found her guts and
courage, and now her tongue behaved, never tripping her up at the sight of a cute guy.

"Married with kids?" he asked.

"No."

He smiled. "Not feeling that big three-oh breathing down your neck?"

"No." For most of the time they'd ever spent together, she'd either wanted to kill him or have his
babies. Apparently that was still the case. God, she'd
been so young, and very naive, and she hated that reminder. If he'd so much as quirked a smile in her direction, she'd have done anything he wanted. Luckily,
he'd never known the power he'd held, and she was no
longer that girl. Nope, she was a twenty-nine-year-old
woman, who absolutely did not want to think about his
smile, and the way it still activated all her good parts.

It'd taken a long time, but painful experience by

painful experience, she'd toughened up, learned to speak up for what she wanted. Mostly, she'd also learned that things worked out much better when *both* parties were enamored.

Not that *that* had happened in a while. After a series of missteps in the man department, mostly due to her own inability to fully connect to someone because when she was so busy with Cece, she'd decided to try something new and had gone off men altogether. Cristina had joined her for a while, but then she'd done the unthinkable and fallen in love with Dustin.

Leaving Lizzy alone on her penis embargo.

Well, not completely alone. Her sister had far more reasons than anyone to give up on men, as she'd just about tried the entire male species, at least all the wild ones anyway. She looked at Jason. "Definitely not feeling the big three-oh breathing down my neck." Her life was just beginning, actually. "Do you know where Dustin is?"

"I don't." He stepped toward her, the light from the lamp bathing him in a soft glow that only emphasized the gorgeousness up close and personal. She tried not to stare at him and failed.

"Are you okay?" he asked.

The closer he got, the harder it was for her to breathe, so no. No, she wasn't okay.

Not by a long shot.

Her legs had turned to overcooked noodles at first sight of him and, despite her resolve, her brain had gone to mush. She could tell herself she'd gotten over him a damn long time ago, but the truth was, if he so much as crooked his pinkie finger in her direction, she was going to regress to that pathetic teenager she'd once been, and melt in a little puddle of longing at his feet.

Lord, this would be so much easier if he'd put some clothes on—

The wind cracked, and with it came an ear splitting *thunk* that shook the house and removed her from her lustful reverie, causing her to jump nearly right out of her skin.

"Just the trees along the side of the house," he murmured, turning his head to look out the window. "Which should have been trimmed." He turned on another light, and…and her brain stuttered to a halt as her eyes ate him up. It was like an opened bag of chips, she couldn't stop herself.

"It's getting bad out there," he said, shifting back to her, his gaze searching her face. "Are you okay?" he repeated.

Oh, man. *Man, oh, man.* He'd changed, too. He was far quieter, far more intense.

And the most devastating—*kind.* When had *that* happened?

She came up to his shoulder. Which meant that her face was right at pec level, and now there was so much light… *Don't look,* she ordered herself. *Don't—*

She looked. And when her gaze dropped, so did her IQ. She couldn't help it, he was just so perfectly made.

He put a finger under her chin and lifted it up. Right. He'd asked her a question. Was she okay? A question that brought her firmly back to the present. And the present was looking tricky. No Dustin meant no SUV, and no SUV meant she'd have to go it alone, and that wasn't going to be easy. "I'm fine. I'm just worried about Cece. It's probably nothing but I just want to go check on her."

"Cece," he said. "Your sister? Troublemaker Cece?"

He remembered. Damn. He was hot *and* sharp, which just didn't seem like a fair distribution of gifts. "She called me last night at work. She said she was fine, no contractions or anything, but now I can't get a hold of her, and—"

His eyes widened. "She's pregnant?"

"Yes. And her cell phone is off. I'm thinking she evacuated, that it's okay, I just need to get a damn life," she said with a self-conscious laugh. "She's growing up and moving on, and I need to do the same, but I just can't go to higher ground and relax until I'm sure." Because a very small part of her couldn't trust her sister to do it, even though she should be able to.

It was asinine. "I can't get to Eastside in my car. I was hoping to borrow Dustin's SUV."

"Okay." Jason shoved his fingers through his hair

and let out a breath, the movement of his arms stretching and flexing all sorts of muscles that pretty much made her mouth dry up. "Where's her husband?"

"There is no husband. The father of her baby ran so fast her head is still spinning. I'd really hoped to find Dustin here."

"I'll have to do."

In truth, he looked a lot like his much kinder, gentler brother. He had dark hair, cut military short. Like Dustin, he had light gray steely eyes that she knew could be warm and playful, or cut like steel.

But unlike Dustin, Jason had an edge, which had only sharpened over time, from his intense gaze to his physique, honed by the military.

"I have a Jeep," he said. "I'll take you to her."

"You?"

"Yes."

"Why?"

He considered her a moment, bemused as he ran a hand down his stubbled jaw. "Because you need a ride?" At her obvious surprise he shook his head. "Jesus, was I that big of an ass?"

She didn't want to go there. No way. "All I need is to borrow your Jeep."

"Ah. So you don't need me. Duly noted. But the Jeep and I are a package deal. Take it or leave it." His smile was tight, and went tighter when her cell phone rang and she pounced on it rather than respond to him.

"Hey," Cristina said. "How goes it?"

"I'm going to go check on Cece."

"Not in this. We were all called in on emergency shifts it's so bad out there."

"I just want to make sure she got out."

"Not by yourself."

"Not exactly." Lizzy glanced at Jason, who was standing where she'd left him, still gloriously half-naked, watching her. "I've got Jason."

He smiled grimly, and nodded his approval of her choice.

"Dustin's Jason?" Cristina asked, letting out a low whistle. "Nice. The guy's a virtual search and rescue team all on his own. But…"

"But what?"

"He's…had a rough few months."

"He looks okay."

He arched a brow in her direction.

More than okay…

"Honey, he looks hot," Cristina corrected with characteristic bluntness and a laugh.

Feeling her face heat, Lizzy turned away from Jason's probing eyes. "I don't see how that's pertinent."

"Then you must have failed Chem 101. It's too bad you have that whole penis embargo going. You going to be able to resist?"

Lizzy risked a look over her shoulder. Jason had leaned back against the wall, arms crossed. Calm and steady.

Look at him, so absolutely at ease in his own skin. She grounded her back teeth together. "Not a problem."

Cristina laughed softly. "Yeah, good luck with that. Call me."

"I will." She slipped her phone into her pocket.

Jason remained silent, his feelings carefully shielded. She had no doubt that he'd be an incredible asset to her out there in the storm, but unfortunately, he was far too dangerous to her mental health. "I want to thank you for offering to help. I appreciate it, but I can do this alone."

He shook his head, annoyance crossing his features. "You always were stubborn as a—"

"Hey."

"—mule," he finished sweetly. As if he was sweet!

"You just got in town," she said, lifting her chin. "I don't want to take up your time." Or hers, staring at his half-naked bod…

He pushed away from the wall. "All I was doing was sleeping. You're going to need help, Lizzy."

"I'll be fine."

"Really? So you know how to drive in weather like this, or how to cross a flooded street? How to get into a flooded building? How to get a pregnant woman out of a flooded building?"

"I'll figure it out."

"I'm going with you."

This was such a bad idea. "Jason—"

"The words are *thank you*."

"Fine. Thank you."

"See, that wasn't so hard." In the old days, he might have added a suggestive smile, a few teasing words, anything to make her blush or stammer or act like an idiot—which she'd done more times than she cared to remember.

But there was none of that now. No mockery. No triumph.

Nothing.

"You asked me if I was okay," she said slowly. "But I feel like I should ask you. Are you—"

"Terrific." He turned away as the house shuddered under the cruel weight of the wind. "Listen, if we're going to do this, we should get moving."

"You think it's going to get worse?"

"Yeah, I do. They're calling for two feet of rain."

"But flooding? Here in Santa Rey?"

"Flash floods can happen anywhere. I should know, I've seen just about every one of them here in the U.S. in the past twelve years." Once again he eyed her scrubs. "You're not dressed for this."

"No, I came from work. I'm a nurse in the E.R."

"Why aren't you a doctor?"

"Long story."

"How about the Cliff's Notes version?"

The Cliff's Notes version was that the world had kicked her ass. Period. She could tell him so, but she didn't like to admit it out loud. "It's not important now." Especially since she still had that dream out in front of her, starting this fall, when she'd enroll in UCLA medical school.

He looked as if maybe he wanted to press the issue, but in the end he simply said, "Do you have a medical bag with you? In case Cece's in labor?"

"As of last night, she wasn't, but yes, I do. In my car."

"And food?"

"Maybe a protein bar or two. Why?"

"Because I'm *starving*." He crouched before a large duffel bag on the floor, which he began rifling through.

She stared at the sleek, smooth muscles in his back, wondering what had happened in the military to erase the happy-go-lucky jock she'd once known. Back then she'd spent hours and hours going over all the what-ifs when it came to him. *What if* he noticed her? *What if* he realized she was the woman of his dreams?

What if...

She'd gotten a lot of mileage out of it all, especially in the deep dark of the night. But in the face of his calm, steady assertiveness, all those what-ifs seemed so very long ago and so very childish. She had only one what-if right now, and that was what if Cece wasn't okay?

"You're really going to take me over there."

"As opposed to sitting on my ass when I know you're worried? Yes, Lizzy, I am."

Okay, now she'd insulted him. Interesting that she could.

She really wished Dustin had been here, Dustin who was so easygoing and laid-back and sweet… "Cristina said your brother's at work."

"Then you really are stuck with me, aren't you." Rising with a pair of jeans in his hand, he settled his calm, quiet eyes on her as his long fingers pulled up the denim. The act seemed shockingly intimate.

Ridiculously so, given that he'd just been standing there in far less. The jeans were loose and clearly beloved old friends, sinking low on his hips as he began to button them up. Stopping halfway, he slid his hand inside to…*adjust*, and as she watched, she felt her face heat. "I'll just…" What? She had no idea so she stood there like an idiot, tongue practically hanging out.

"You'll…?"

"No idea," she whispered, giving up.

Seeming amused as he finished buttoning, he gave her a glimpse of the younger Jason she'd once known.

Again the house shuddered, and she braced. The sound of the driving rain was relentless as he pulled a T-shirt on over that torso, which could have been on the cover of any fitness magazine. He added an old hooded sweatshirt to his ensemble, then crouched again to dig through his bag for socks.

Then he turned and eyed her scrubs.

She knew they were unflattering, not to mention wet from her dash from the car, and clinging to her. "Those won't work," he said, and tossed her some clothes. "These are dry."

She caught them to her. "I'm not going to take your things."

"Yes, you are," he said in the quiet authoritative voice he probably used on the job and had people jumping to obey him.

But it didn't move her to follow his order as much as it…excited her. Yes, she was that badly off that a quiet, confident, masculine voice could excite her.

She really needed to get sex more often. Too bad she tended to self-destruct her relationships. She looked out the window. Daylight was trying valiantly to break through. The rain was still coming down so thickly it looked like a virtual sheet of water pouring from the sky. "Changing isn't going to help for long."

"You're shivering." He also tossed over a set of rain gear. "You won't be any good to me out there if you're not at least warm."

She wouldn't be any good to *him?* "Okay, now just a minute. I—"

"Your sister isn't the only one who might be in trouble, Lizzy. I can guarantee it. We might run into people out there who need our help. You're going to want to be able to give it. Where exactly does Cece live?"

"Third and Cove. Problem is they're evacuating Eastside because the flooding is already bad."

"Then we need to hurry." He straightened and looked at her. Waiting.

Oh, no. No, no, no. Hell to the no was she

going to change right here in front of him. Sure, there'd been all those times when she'd secretly— very secretly—dreamed about such things, but those days were long gone.

So long gone.

This man, with his steely, unreadable eyes and grim mouth, with his big, tough body braced for whatever came his way, wasn't the stuff of girlhood dreams.

He was all man.

Complicated, edgy man, and no longer someone she fantasized about.

And maybe if she kept saying that, she'd believe it. "Fine. I'll change."

At that, he gave her his full attention, his entire body emitting so much testosterone she could hardly lock her knees. "Not right here, of course," she corrected coolly, and stiffening her traitorous knees, she stepped around him, heading down the hall to his bathroom, shutting the door behind her.

She forced herself to shake off the sensual haze and turned to stare at herself in the mirror, sucking in a breath at the sight that greeted her.

Flushed cheeks.

Glassy eyes.

"Stop it," she whispered, and quickly locked the bathroom door, not letting herself wonder who exactly she was locking it against—her or him.

3

JASON WATCHED HER GO and let out a long breath. He couldn't believe it. Shy, carefully controlled Lizzy Mann, with the sweet-smelling brunette hair, and those melting chocolate eyes, the ones that had once revealed everything she thought every time she thought it, here in his house.

When they'd been young, she'd been a danger to herself for no reason other than he always knew exactly how she felt about everything: school, life, *him*.

But she'd be a danger to *him* now, because they were adults, and incredibly enough there was something there between them, something undeniable. Actually, it'd always been there, and it had nothing at all to do with her sweet, curvy body.

Okay, it had a lot to do with that curvy body, but it was more, far more. Once upon a time she'd stimulated his brain, and she'd been the first girl to do so.

And now she was no girl.

Which was bad timing all around, because since Matt's death, he'd been pretty screwed up and wasn't ready for a relationship. Hell, he wasn't ready for real life. He had no idea what he wanted anymore, or even what was important to him.

Not with the damn rug yanked out from beneath his feet.

A gust of wind hit the house with what felt like a battering ram, immediately followed by the sound of glass shattering, and a short, startled scream. He whipped down the hallway just as the lights flickered once and went out. *"Lizzy?"*

The bathroom door opened as he craned his neck to see the broken glass, which had come from the bedroom across the hall. The window directly over his bed had blown in.

"It just scared me," she said, following his gaze. "Sorry."

With the driving rain the only sound around them, he suddenly became aware he'd pulled her to his side.

It'd been instinctive to do so, simply about concern, but that was draining quickly, replaced by something else entirely as his hand slowly moved up and down her arm.

Adrenaline. It was churning inside him now because of the blown window. Hell, it was still in him from his last mission.

From coming home again.

From being awoken after his first deep sleep in... forever.

From losing Matt.

It'd been a long time since he'd touched a woman, held one. Since someone had touched him in return.

Too long.

Knowing it, knowing damn well he was treading on thin ice, he bent his head for the simple pleasure of rubbing his jaw against hers.

She swallowed hard and, against his chest, he felt her hand settle, then slowly fist into his sweatshirt, not to push him away but to pull him in even tighter as she shivered.

"You're cold," he whispered, skimming both hands up her slim spine now.

"No. Not cold."

God. God, he wanted…

This.

Her.

More.

Then her focus dropped to his mouth, and her lips parted, and that was all he needed. The sign that she felt it, too, this crazy heat. She wanted him to kiss her.

With that his only thought, he leaned in and did just that, all coherent thought going out the broken window as she opened her mouth beneath his and tentatively, sweetly, hesitantly, met his tongue with hers. It made him groan in sheer pleasure because, God, her mouth. She might have grown up and toughened up on the outside, but on the inside she was still soft and sweet, still just a little shy.

He'd take that, he'd take all she wanted to give and

to that end, he cupped her head in one palm, running his other hand down her back to nudge her even closer. She crawled right in, right up against him as if made for the spot, accompanying the movement with a little purr from deep in her throat. He loved the way she didn't keep her hands to herself, loved how they ran up his arms, over his chest, around his neck and into his hair.

Loved.

It.

But then more glass fell from the bedroom windowpane, flying into the room, the hallway, hitting the floor around them with a musical tinkling sound that had them tearing free of each other.

Breathing almost harder than the wind outside, she stared up at him, mouth wet, eyes wide. "What was that?"

"A damn good kiss." He expected her to pull clear, but she surprised him when instead, she leaned back in and pressed her face to his throat. Not breathing any more steadily than she, he wrapped her up in his arms again, cupping the bare nape of her neck. Indulging himself, he bent his head and inhaled her in.

"Are you…smelling my hair?"

"Yes." He did it again, drawing in her scent. "God, you smell amazing. I've smelled nothing but dust and other guys for so long I just want to wrap myself up in you." But the house was taking a beating. He needed to cover up the window openings to prevent more damage…

"Do you have a sheet of plywood for that window?"

"I hope so." The tree just outside his bedroom was whipping back and forth, dangerously close to the blown-in window. Glass shards lay across the bed, on top of the sheets and blankets where he'd been only a few minutes ago. "Good thing you woke me up."

"You were sleeping there?" Lizzy asked, sounding horrified as she pulled free.

"Yeah." He shut the bedroom door, closing off the wind and rain freely flying in, and looked at her.

Her hair had been demurely pulled back into a low ponytail when she'd first arrived, but was loose now. The dark honey strands fell to her shoulders, with long side swept bangs framing her face.

Her mouth was still wet.

Which made him want to kiss her again. Forget the storm beating the shit out of his house, forget Cece out there in it—

Okay, he couldn't forget that. He needed to get his mind off the fantasy currently running in high def in his head, the one that had him pushing Lizzy to the wall and kissing her again until she didn't look so worried, and then taking that kiss to its natural course, which involved no clothes and her crying out his name as she came.

But life was rarely that good to him.

So he turned her back to the bathroom door, where the only window was narrow and high up inside the shower. "Change. I'm going to the garage to look for plywood."

"The electricity is out."

"Yeah, it's probably going to stay out for a good long time, too." What the hell. He slid his fingers into her hair again, smoothing it back off her face for the sheer pleasure of feeling her warm skin beneath his palm.

She caught his hand in hers. "Before," she said. "When I screamed? You came running."

He looked into her eyes, and there was a long beat between them, where the icy air didn't seem cold at all but rather shimmering with heat.

The heat coming from them.

He'd survived the past two months by putting aside emotions and feelings. It was a tactic that had served him well.

But he was feeling now, big-time.

"I slay my own dragons these days, Jason," she said softly, and went back into the bathroom.

At the sound of the lock hitting home, he smiled grimly. She didn't need him. Message received.

He found no plywood in the garage, which meant that the room was going to be a wreck before this was over. Hoping that would be the extent of the damage, he came back into the kitchen and took another food foray. This time, in the dubious light of the morning, he found a box of crackers and Cheez Whiz.

Worked for him.

Loading up crackers and stuffing them into his mouth, he called his mom. She answered on the first ring, breathless and excited. "My baby! Honey, are you back?"

"Yeah." At the sound of her love practically pouring through the phone line, he let out a breath and a reluctant smile. "You okay?"

"Oh, sweetheart, I'm fine. Tell me you're coming here so I can fatten you up and see for myself you're in one piece."

"I'm in one piece."

"Are you sure? Because the last time we talked, you were in such a bad place—"

That had been right after Matt's death. He'd been a mess. "Mom." He paused, his throat tightening. "I'm good."

"I'll be the judge of that. When will I see you?"

"Soon as this storm is over. Is Shelly okay? The house? You both safe?"

"We aren't flooding, we're both staying put, and we're fine. I love you, Jason."

"Love you, too, Mom."

"Prove it and get up here as soon as you can."

He promised to do that and shut his phone, resuming the stuffing of his face with the crackers and Cheez Whiz until Lizzy came into the room.

He still couldn't wrap his brain around it. She'd once had a way of looking at him, of seeing things in him that had made him uncomfortable, to say the least. He hadn't liked looking into those sweet orbs and seeing himself reflected back, because he'd never liked what he'd seen.

Of course she was no longer looking at him the way she used to. She'd learned to temper her emotions. And she'd gotten good at it, too, because she was staring right at him and he had absolutely no idea what she was thinking.

She wore his sweats, which swam on her. Covered from chin to toe, she was now shapeless, which was good. Now maybe he could forget how she'd looked when he'd first flicked on the light, when her thin scrubs had been drenched through and clinging to her curves. "Warmer?" he asked.

"Yes. Thanks." She narrowed in on the jar in his hand. "Breakfast of champions?"

He turned the jar in his palm and read the ingredients. "Hey, it's got five percent of my daily required protein. Practically a vitamin."

She actually smiled, and whoa baby, that was new. He hadn't seen many smiles out of her in their high school years. She'd been too shy, too reserved. The smile transformed her face, and while he stared stupidly at her, she came close and read over his shoulder. "It's ninety-five percent fat, Jase."

Jase. No one had called him that since...well, since her, and he laughed, his first in a good long time. "Ready to roll?"

"Yeah. Listen——" She broke off to glance over his shoulder, at the window above the sink, and her entire body went tense. *"Move!"* she cried, adding a shove packed with surprising strength for a little thing, taking them both down to the tile floor with a bone-jarring thud.

Above them the kitchen window shattered, spraying in glass and wind and water, all of which rained down over the top of them.

Jason managed not to bash his head on the floor as he circled his arms around Lizzy, trying to cushion her fall but not quite succeeding. Lying there flat on his back with her sprawled over the top of him, he tightened his grip when she gasped and wriggled. "Don't move," he demanded. "The glass." He slid his fingers into her hair and stared up at her, searching her face. "Are you okay?"

She craned her neck to look behind them, where he'd been standing, where the majority of the glass had hit. Rain was flying in freely now, pushed by the brutal wind. The branch that had broken the window shimmied and danced in the opening. "That almost got you," she breathed.

"Well, it didn't, thanks to you." He turned her head back to his. "And do you ever answer a question?"

"I'm fine. And you're not," she said, pointing to where blood was blooming through the material of his shirt from a slice on his upper arm. She started to push herself up but her grimace tipped him off and he held her still, reaching for her hand, which was also cut.

He sat up, which meant that she was sitting, too, straddling him. In the back of his mind he registered the fact that it was a very nice position to be in as he ran his gaze over her carefully, looking for— "Damn." Another cut. Gently he ran a finger over her cheekbone, which was beginning to bleed. "Just a nick, though."

"I'm okay." Using nothing but thigh muscles, she stood, then reached down with her uninjured hand to pull him up. Very carefully she brushed the glass from him, until he grabbed her wrist and moved them both from the shattered window, back into the living room. "Sit," he said, gesturing to the couch, going for his first-aid kit from his bag.

"I will if you will."

"So you're still stubborn," he noted, amused at both of them.

"As a mule. And I'm the nurse, remember?" She grabbed the first-aid kit from him as he sat next to her.

"I'm a trained medic." He grabbed it back, holding it over her head.

"So, what, brute strength trumps brains?"

"Look at you," he murmured. "You've grown claws. I'm so proud."

"I call it a backbone."

His smile faded. "Ah, Lizzy. You always had that."

And while she stared at him in surprise, he got to

work cleaning, gauzing and wrapping up her palm with medical tape. He swiped her cheek with antiseptic, then let her repeat the favor on him.

"If we're done playing doctor…" she murmured when she'd finished.

He had no idea what it said about him that he loved this new version of her, all tough and no longer so reserved. Once upon a time she'd stirred protectiveness and affection within him, and definitely the normal horniness of a teenage boy. All of which he'd hidden.

The woman she'd grown into stirred a hell of a lot more. But what shocked him was that he didn't feel like hiding from any of it.

"What are you grinning about?" she asked.

Other than he had his first hard-on in eight weeks? "I like this Lizzy."

"You don't know this Lizzy."

True. But as he looked out the window into the sheer destruction of the day, he had a feeling he was going to get to know her pretty quickly. "I knew you once."

"For a minute."

"Longer than that," he chided gently. "We were friends."

She laughed. "Friends? We weren't friends, Jason. I did your English papers, and you…"

"I…?"

"You were a jerk."

"Not *all* the time."

"*All* the time."

"Come on. What about the day I taught you to kiss after that idiot Paul Drucker said you kissed like a poodle?"

"I try not to remember that day," she said bitterly.

"I don't know. It was a pretty good day for me."

She turned away. "I don't want to talk about it."

"About which, the fact that we kissed behind the bleachers until you had it right? Or how afterward, you—"

She sent him a glacial glance over her shoulder. "I said I don't want to talk about it." She paused, then let out a sigh. "But thanks for teaching me how to kiss."

"You are most welcome."

"You know…" She narrowed her eyes. "Now that I think about it, the whole teaching process took a lot longer than it should have."

"Did it?"

"Yes."

He smiled. "You kissed like heaven, Lizzy, from the get-go. Paul was an idiot *and* an ass."

"So you only pretended I needed kissing tutoring? Why?"

"Hello, I was seventeen."

With an annoyed sound, she walked away.

Yeah, he'd been an ass, but only because of what had happened next, the thing she didn't want to talk about, and for the first time in all these years, he remembered, and felt regret. "Lizzy—"

"I'm going."

"We've been through this. If you go, I go."

"I'm sure you had other plans today."

"Yeah," he agreed readily enough. "I had a whole list—sleep, food and sex." He smiled tightly. "Not that I was going to get any of that. There's nothing good to eat here, and as it's just me, sex wouldn't be much fun."

She looked at him. "Is this what you do in the Guard?" she asked. "Rescue people?"

"A lot, yeah." Or in the case of Matt, not.

"Are you going back to it?"

"That seems to be the million-dollar question."

She let out a half smile, full of sympathy. "Still decompressing?"

"Yeah." More than she could possibly know, and it was a reminder, a cold slap of hard reality that he had decisions to make for a future he didn't want to face. So it was him who turned away this time, needing to break eye contact, needing to not let her in his head.

She was quiet as he bent to put on his shoes. "When we had the big fires here last year, I worked four straight days without much more than a few catnaps. My entire life was the E.R., treating the firefighters, the victims, and when I finally got off duty and out into the parking lot where I'd left my car, I had the weirdest thing happen."

He straightened. "What?"

"I broke down." She lifted a shoulder. "I just sat

on the curb and cried like a baby for half an hour. I have no idea why."

He could picture it. Hell, he'd lived it. "That was sheer exhaustion, Lizzy."

"Yes. After only *four* days of hell."

Knowing where she was going with this, he shook his head. "Don't."

She walked toward him. "I have to." Her gaze touched over each of his features, feeling like a caress. "I felt that way after only four days of adrenaline and fear and craziness, so I can only imagine what it's like for you after years."

"I'm fine."

"Yes," she agreed. "Very fine."

Her words made him want to smile but he held back because she didn't stop moving until they were toe to toe, until she'd once again put a hand on his chest.

Clearly she wasn't finished with hacking at his hard-earned self-control.

"I'm sure there's a transition period," she said very quietly, giving him something he hadn't had any of and didn't want because it ripped at that control more than anything else could—sympathy. "Between what you've been doing, and being here…" Her hand slid over his chest until she laid her palm right over his heart, which was not nearly as steady as he'd have liked. "I imagine there's a disconnect. A gap."

She had no idea. "The size of the equator," he agreed, not thrilled that his voice came out low and hoarse.

She was quiet another moment, then reached for his hand. "Don't worry, Jase, I'm sure it'll come to you, what you want to do."

Well, he was glad she was sure. Because he wasn't.

The moment broken, she dropped her hands from him and turned away.

He slipped into his rain gear while she did the same. He put two first-aids kits inside his backpack and shouldered it.

"Two?" she asked.

"Who knows what we'll need."

"There's only a couple of inches so far."

"Yeah, but even one inch in the wrong place can cause flash flooding, which can bring walls of water ten to twenty feet high. Trust me, there's a whole town out there thinking this is no big deal, but it can turn into one in seconds. Plus, if we find Cece and she's in labor—"

"When." Her voice was unyielding as she corrected him. "*When* we find her."

"If she's out there," he promised, "we'll find her."

"Yeah." She broke eye contact, getting busy with adjusting her rain poncho.

Reaching out, he lifted her chin, ran the pad of his thumb over the cut on her cheek. "We'll find her."

She nodded, hugging herself in all those layers. He had to work hard not to add his arms to the mix. He'd come here wanting to feel nothing, but look at him, feeling emotions all over the place. Shaking his head at himself, he opened the door and, as the wind and rain drafted in, reached for her hand.

"Jason?"

"Yeah?"

She looked up into his eyes. "Thank you."

He took in the craziness of the storm. Power lines down. Trees doubled over. Several inches of rain sloshing at the curbs. A flash of Matt's face came to him, and his gut tightened. "Don't thank me yet."

4

CECE MANN PACED THROUGH the contraction. Miraculously, it was her first real pain, meaning it was the first one to make her want to twist some guy's nuts off.

Actually, make that *every* guy's nuts off.

Not so miraculously, she didn't like this whole labor business, not one little bit. "Okay," she said to her belly, rubbing the insidious tightness swirling through her gut. "I need you to give me a little more time. Can you do that, hold on for your momma? Please?"

The pain actually faded, and she let out a breath. "Thank you. Because I promised your aunt Lizzy we weren't in labor yet, so let's just keep that promise, okay?"

She'd read in one of the hundred books that Lizzy had brought her that even once her water broke she still had twenty-four hours before things went wrong.

That hadn't happened yet so that was good. "Real good," she whispered, with no idea if she was talking to herself or the baby, but she thought, *hoped,* if she said it out loud, it would make it so.

She moved to the window of the second floor of the

small condo she'd rented a few months ago—her first true sign of independence. Every day the place gave her a sense of panic—the expenses were a weight about as heavy as the baby—and also a glorious, heady sense of pride. She was making it, on her own...

She looked out into the wildest weather she'd ever seen, and had a moment before she reverted and wished her sister was here. Lizzy would know what to do. She always knew what to do. She was Cece's lifeline, and had been nearly all her life.

She'd come, Cece knew, assuring herself, even though she'd told her not to. Lizzy would come when she got off work, and being as bossy as she was, she'd probably demand they go straight to the hospital.

Which might actually be a good idea. She had a feeling it was time. All she needed was a ride. If she had a neighbor she trusted, that'd be one thing. But she'd never been good with trust. Unless it was a gorgeous guy. Those she'd trusted too easily, and look where that had gotten her.

The next pain hit her unawares and left her reeling. "Oh, shit," she whispered. This was going to suck golf balls, and forget being a grown-up, she wanted Lizzy. She tried calling her again, to admit that maybe she *was* in labor, but her damn cell phone went dead.

And she had no electricity to charge it.

Oh, God.

Screw not trusting a neighbor, she needed one. Problem was, the condo on her right was empty and for sale. She'd known someone had just bought the condo on her left, but she hadn't yet seen any sign of life. She imagined waddling over there, knocking, then greeting whoever answered with, "Hi, there. Ever delivered a baby before?"

The thought made her shudder.

No. No strangers. It was bad enough the father-to-be was a stranger, coaxing her into his badass truck one night, dumping her he next.

God, she hated the helplessness. She thought about walking to the hospital. From here it was only two miles, but in the storm, with contractions, that might as well have been a marathon. Besides, it was too risky. She could fall. She could get halfway there and go into the final stages of labor, alone. That thought terrified her even more than having a stranger help her.

Karma was such a bitch. "I've turned my life around," she reminded the room. "I stopped finding trouble. I stopped letting it find me." She'd even gotten a real job. She was going back to school, taking classes at the junior college. She was making it all work, for the first time in her life, taking charge of her own destiny instead of letting it rule her. "I am!"

But Karma wasn't listening.

"I promise," she whispered to God, to Lizzy, to whoever listened to such recklessly whispered promises, "if I get out of this mess, this *last* mess, I'll keep it together. I will. Just give me one little break!"

She felt a funny sort of pop, then the warm wetness on her thighs and, cringing, she looked down.

With a sigh, she shook her head. "Not the 'break' I meant, but thanks, Karma. Thanks a whole hell of a lot."

LIZZY GASPED AT the slap of cold rain as she and Jason ran through the storm toward her car. There she grabbed her bag and they turned to Jason's Jeep. A heavy gust had her staggering backward, fighting gravity, but Jason was behind her. "Sorry," she gasped, her back plastered to his chest.

He merely slid an arm around her waist, helping her secure her balance. His feet were planted. He was a solid rock behind her.

But she was a rock, too.

And well used to managing on her own. She struggled to regain her footing, determined to do so, extremely aware of the fact that he stayed right at her back until she did, only dropping his arm when she nodded.

Water ran down her in rivulets, making her grateful he'd given her the rain gear, and she stared in disbelief at the street, which appeared to be under a sheet of water.

"It's rising fast," Jason said, voice raised over the wind.

Visibility was just about nil. The air was thick with

rain and whatever the wind was tossing around—tree branches, sand, dirt, lawn furniture…

Jason helped her into the Jeep, his hands on her waist, her hips. A light touch. An impersonal touch. He'd have helped anyone.

But she absorbed the feeling of his hands on her, the one on her spine, the one on her hip, both coaxing a shiver from her that had nothing to do with the icy air, and she realized something horrifying.

Her secret little crush, the one buried deep inside her, had renewed itself.

She watched as he came around the driver's side, moving with the easy grace of a man who'd been trained and honed into a physical prowess she could only dream of.

He was as drenched as she, his hair dark and shiny, his lashes inky and spiky over those solemn and determined eyes.

Being wet suited him.

He tossed the backpack to the backseat and turned on the engine. "What?" he asked, meeting her gaze.

"Nothing." At least she wanted it to be nothing. She put on her seat belt as he flicked on the radio, searching for local news. "Jason…I realize I'm completely overreacting. In my heart, I know Cece's fine."

"But you have to see for yourself. I get it. It's your hang-up, not hers. I feel the same about my baby sister."

She let out a low laugh. "I've just been in control for so long, I'm having trouble letting go."

"I get that, too. Loss of control sucks."

She got the feeling he was speaking from personal experience, but he turned his attention to the rain that pelted the roof, only partly drowned out by the heater, which he cranked full blast. She blinked out through the windshield wipers whooshing back and forth. The ocean to their left was a frothy mess, the waves higher than she'd ever seen, splashing up and over the entire beach and onto the parking lot across the street, a sight that made her breath catch.

"Evacuations are in effect from Eastside to Sixth now," the deejay said. "Repeat—the streets on the Eastside are flooding. Stay off the roads from East-side to Main. Head to higher ground from the west."

She looked at Jason. "There's no reason for both of us to risk our necks."

"You're going to piss me off with that."

"Just saying."

"Well, stop. Just saying." He shook his head. "You always did have a problem asking for help."

"Me? I never needed your help. It was your teacher who made you come to me for tutoring."

"Well, I guess that makes us both stubborn asses then." He pulled out his vibrating cell phone and looked at the ID. "It's Dustin." He flipped open the phone. "Yeah, yeah, I'm home two days early. You order all this rain for me?" He listened a minute then looked out the window, away from Lizzy, his shoulders tensing. "If you've talked to Mom, you know I'm fine— No, I don't want to talk about Matt. *Jesus.*" He glanced back at Lizzy. "Yeah, I've got her. She came to the house, looking for you— Uh-huh, that's the plan." He paused. "Okay. I'll tell her." He closed his phone, shoved it into his pocket and put the Jeep into gear.

"Tell me what?"

"Dustin's at the hospital, part of the roof blew off and the backup generator failed. They're transporting patients to San Luis Obispo Memorial, he'll be busy for hours. So you really are stuck with me." He looked at her as if expecting further objection. When she didn't say anything, he pulled out of the driveway and turned right.

Except they needed to go left to get into town. "Where are we going?"

He downshifted to merge onto the main highway above town. "Keeping out of the low areas." There were no other cars on the road that they could see, which was just as well, as every time he turned, the rear-end of the Jeep fishtailed. He kept his focus straight forward, his body seemingly relaxed, but she knew it was taking all his concentration to keep them on the road.

"According to Dustin," he said. "Main Street is a water slide. The Jeep might be able to plow through."

Or might not.

He didn't say it, he didn't need to.

"A foot of floodwater will float most vehicles. Two will plain and simple just carry us away. I don't know how much water we're dealing with right now, but it's clearly rising. We'll go the long way around, get on the highway and come in from the other side. It's an extra two miles, but on higher ground."

Okay, smart move. "Thank you."

He flicked her a glance. "Are you going to thank me every step of the way?"

"Maybe."

His lips twitched as he drove down the highway at ten miles per hour instead of the speed limit of sixty-five miles per hour. Still, the water shot up from beneath the tires in two matching plumes along either side of the vehicle. Lizzy leaned forward as if that would help her see better. It didn't. She had no idea how he could tell where they were going. "Maybe you'll be thanking *me* for something by the end of the day."

"Yeah?" He looked amused. "Like what?"

Well, he had her there.

"Maybe you're right," he said after a minute. "Maybe you'll save my sorry ass again, like you did with the window. Or better yet, tell me what the hell to do with my sorry ass." He offered a self-deprecatory smile, letting her in on the joke, and a reluctant one tugged at her mouth, as well. "Look at that," he murmured. "That smile sure looks good on you."

"I smile plenty." Okay, maybe not plenty. "When it's warranted."

"Yeah, see, the thing about smiling is that it's supposed to happen whenever and wherever, not just 'when warranted.'"

"There are inappropriate times."

"Like?"

"Like this. This is an inappropriate smile time. It's a serious situation."

"There's always a serious situation." His smile faded. "It's what you make of it."

Wasn't that the truth. She could see in his eyes, from the sudden haunted hollowness in them, that he was once again speaking from experience. Like her, he'd lost his father young, but unlike her and Cece, he still had great family support. He'd grown up with a sense of responsibility, even giving back with his job. In fact, his job was the *ultimate* give-back, putting his life on the line for his country. "I think it's amazing, what you do."

"No different than you," he said.

"I'm an R.N. in the emergency room, Jason. We both know I'm a dime a dozen."

"That's not true." He flicked her a glance. "And you don't really feel that way."

No. No, she didn't. In the beginning, she'd resented being a nurse instead of a doctor, but truthfully, she'd come to love her job. It gave her a sense of purpose, a belief that she was here for a reason, and yeah, there'd been times when she'd desperately needed that belief. In the fall, things would change. She'd be going into the unknown. "How do you know what I feel?"

"Let's see. We're driving into a storm that we should be running from because someone might or might not need you."

"It's not any someone. It's my sister."

"Come on. You'd be doing this for a perfect stranger."

"And you *are*," she pointed out. "You're doing this for a perfect stranger."

"I'm doing it for you."

She looked at him and saw the truth. Much as she wanted to think of him as that laid-back kid he'd once been because it helped her keep her distance, she really couldn't.

Because the man he'd turned into was amazing.

"More flood warnings," the deejay announced. "Mandatory evacuations for all of Eastside. Head out toward the west, via Highway 1 or 101. The shelters are at Madison Junior High and the Huntington Library."

"It's the fires we had this past summer," Lizzy said. "They destroyed the natural landscape, and now we've got too much rain. We'll be lucky not to get mudslides, as well."

They'd had mudslides ten years ago, which had washed out dozens of homes. She'd been nineteen at the time, trying to raise Cece, still grieving her parents, and terrified at the devastating destruction the slides had brought.

"Don't you think Cece'll head to one of the designated shelters?" Jason asked.

"Yeah." But the truth was, Cece didn't do what she was told. She had a little authority problem. Okay, a big authority problem. They were working on that.

"You just want to make sure."

"Yeah."

He slid her a look. "So who checks on you?"

"I don't need checking on."

"Come on. Everyone does once in a while."

"Really?" she asked. "Even you?"

"My mom will be calling me even when I'm old and gray. So why aren't you a doctor, Lizzy?"

"Things came up."

"Things…like checking on your sister?"

"You're a funny guy, Jason."

"I try." He took the last exit for Santa Rey. Eastside. The road took a natural dip down and the car hydroplaned. "Shit," he muttered. "Hold on."

Lizzy bit her lower lip and gripped the dash as he fought for control and barely found it just as the road curved. The back end of the Jeep fishtailed, then the tires lost their grip.

They went sliding directly toward a grove of trees, one of which had lost several large branches, which were blocking the road.

The brakes didn't catch.

They spun away from the fallen branches, but Jason swore viciously as the car whipped around toward the trees themselves.

A cold shot of horror skittered down Lizzy's spine and she heard herself gasp in terror as they flew at the two massive trees, and then—

Jerked to a sudden, neck-snapping stop, with the nose of the Jeep a mere inch from two of the biggest tree trunks she'd ever seen, both of which filled the entire windshield.

5

IN THE SHOCKED SILENCE, with the Jeep still rocking from the sudden stop, Lizzy felt Jason whip toward her, his eyes dark and fiercely protective. "Lizzy."

"Present," she whispered, still staring at the big, fat, thick tree trunks. "That was…adrenaline-pumping."

"Yeah." He put his hands on her arm and turned her to him.

Oddly enough, her gaze went—inappropriately—to his mouth. She couldn't help it. "Another inch, and we'd have been kissing those tree trunks."

He let out a low laugh as his hand traveled up her spine, coaxing her even closer. "We'd have been swallowing them whole."

She didn't resist the pressure of his hand, but willingly shifted to him, nearly melting when his fingers swept up and then down again, this time finding their way beneath all the layers she wore.

His fingers were sure and warm, a sweet shock to cover the nasty one of the near accident.

"You okay?" he murmured.

"Yes." And getting more okay by the second. His

face was so close to hers that the roughness of his jaw brushed the skin of her cheek. She closed her eyes to better absorb it, not even trying to figure out what the hell was wrong with her that this languid sensuality could take her over here, now. "Jason?"

"Uh-huh." His lips barely grazed hers once, and then again, and she leaned helplessly into him, seeking more than just the promise of a kiss, and getting it as his tongue took itself on an erotic foray in her mouth.

He kissed different than anyone else she'd ever kissed. He kissed as if it wasn't the way to a prize, but the prize itself, and she could have kissed him forever. His lips were slow and searching, hard and then not, causing a rising heat within her that unbelievably, given where they were and what they had yet to do, had a languid pleasure unfurling from deep within her. She became extremely aware of the fact that she was trying to crawl into his lap just as he lifted her with astonishing ease, bringing her over him, his mouth never leaving hers, delving deeper, longer, while she did her best to swallow him whole.

In the back of her mind, she knew this was simply pent-up fear and adrenaline, but she didn't care. She wanted his tongue, she wanted his body. Hell, she wanted to throw the seat back and feel him sink into her aching flesh. She wanted it all. It was as if something had been cut loose, and even knowing she had the storm, the craziness of the day to blame for it, deep down she also knew it was something more.

It was Jason.

For a woman who prided herself on her ready and able control, *had* to have that ready and able to control, she was losing it big-time here, but what was turning her on more than anything else was that she wasn't alone.

Jason, who also lived off his famed control, was fighting for self-restraint every bit as much as she, and losing the battle. His breath was coming in short, ragged pants, his hands gripping her tight as his mouth made its hungry way along her throat. Beneath her, he was hard as a rock, and she wanted him so much, wanted this more than she'd imagined she could, and for that very reason she had to stop.

"Jason." Her voice came out a rough whisper and she had to clear her throat and try again. *"Jason."*

He went still, then slowly lifted his head, his eyes dark and slumberous as if waking from a dream. The sight of the tree trunks in the windshield sobered him up pretty quick, and she crawled off him and back to her seat.

Still eyeing the tree trunks, he caught her wrist and brought her palm to his lips. "That really was uncomfortably close."

Yeah, it was. "Thanks for being such a good driver."

His eyes met hers, the amusement peeking through

the heat. "How do you know that I wasn't referring to the fact that we nearly—"

"Oh. Um. Yeah, that, too."

He let out a low laugh. "You've got nerves of steel, Lizzy. Are you sure you're all right?"

Let's see. If she discounted the fact that her body was howling, *howling,* for him to finish her off, then maybe, *maybe* she was all right. "Yes. I'm sure."

"The roads are getting tricky."

"Can we make it?"

"I hope so." He craned his neck right and left, looking around them. "Going to have to move those branches blocking the road first. Wait here."

"You'll need help." She hopped out into the wild storm with him, the rain and wind pummeling them as her feet sank into nearly six inches of water.

"Go back," Jason yelled.

She eyed the grove of trees lining the road on the left where the Jeep was. On the right was nothing but a rushing river of runoff, which was rising high and fast. It wouldn't be much longer before that rushing water overtook the road entirely. Knowing it, she ran after Jason, to where he was dragging two of the branches to the side. She reached for another and tugged.

And didn't budge it.

She reset her feet, squinted into the rain stinging her eyes and tried again.

Nothing.

She closed her eyes and strained, putting everything into it, and suddenly the branch lifted with ease. Shocked, she opened her eyes and met Jason's from the other side, who took the thing from her and tossed it aside as if it weighed nothing.

Then he grabbed her hand and they ran back to the Jeep. Inside, he leaned back, breathing hard. "I'm going to need more Cheez Whiz."

"Really?" She swiped rain from her eyes. "Because that looked pretty effortless."

He slid her a look. He had water running down his face, his eyes deep and dark as they met hers.

"I couldn't even budge that thing," she pointed out.

"Are you going to say thank-you again?" he asked. "Because I'd rather receive my thanks in the form of food. Or…" Without moving a muscle on his face, he somehow managed to change his expression from exhausted to wickedly naughty.

She actually laughed. "I'm *not* thanking you with sex."

"Well, damn."

She pulled out an energy bar from her bag and handed it to him. "A peace offering."

He stuffed half the bar into his mouth, handing her the other half. "You've grown up, Lizzy, and toughened up. That's going to be a good thing today."

She looked at him, really looked, knowing he'd grown up, too. Entirely.

"Ready?" he asked quietly.

Even more disconcerting than the fact that he'd grown up and moved on? The realization that she hadn't. Nope. She still wanted the same thing her teenage self had wanted—him. Preferably naked and on a platter.

"Lizzy?"

"Yeah. I'm ready." For far more than she cared to admit.

JASON THRUST THE Jeep into gear and hit the gas, getting his head into the game. Or trying to. It shouldn't have been an issue, but hearing Lizzy say his name with such easy familiarity tended to make him think of things he shouldn't have been thinking.

But then the tires spun uselessly, bringing him back.

"Try Reverse," she said.

He did. More of the same.

"Oh, boy." She looked out into the storm. "You don't by any chance have any kitty litter in the back, which we could use as traction beneath the tires?"

"Good idea, but no." He craned his neck and looked out the window, knowing there was only one thing to do. "Come here."

"What?"

"Scoot over here."

"You want me to drive? Sure," she said, game. "But I might not be able to get us out any more than you could."

He let out a low laugh. He loved her strength, her attitude. "No, I'm going to go out and push, and you're going to—"

"Pop the Jeep out of Neutral and into Reverse, then hit the gas and keep it moving," she guessed. Accurately. "Bad idea, though. The Jeep might slip and hit you."

"Yeah, if you could not do that, that'd be great."

"That's not funny."

"Just get the Jeep moving, I'll handle the rest."

"Okay, but once I do get it going, I won't be able to stop or we'll get stuck again." She met his gaze. "Run fast."

"Will do." He hopped out and into driving rain. Making his way through the mud to the front of the Jeep, he braced himself, then looked through the windshield and met Lizzy's calm gaze, very glad that if he had to do this, he was with someone who could hold their own. "On three," he said. "One. Two. *Three*—" He shoved, and she got it into Reverse and hit the gas, steering out of the ditch. He ran after her, slogging through the water to hop into the passenger seat. "Nice."

"This is probably a good time to tell you, I haven't driven a stick in ten years."

Laughing, he swiped the water from his face. "Then extra nice."

The water was rushing down the road with them, almost faster than the Jeep. He knew they didn't have much longer before any car on the road wouldn't be drivable, this vehicle included. In fact, he'd consider them damn lucky if they made it to Cece's. "We might have to stay at the condo and ride this out."

"Yeah." Her attention was on the road. "If she's not in labor that won't be a problem."

And if she was, and they had to evacuate quickly... "We'll handle it," he promised, just as he saw another huge tree, this one down across the road ahead. Lizzy saw it, too, and hit the brakes and the clutch together.

"Not so hard," he said quickly. "Let up a little."

Too late. The tires didn't grab, and they went into their second slide.

"Ohmigod," she gasped. "I'm sorry, hold on..."

"Steer into the slide, Lizzy. Steer into it—"

"I'm trying!" They spun in a full three-hundred-and-sixty circle and missed their second tree by inches.

In the ensuing silence, Lizzy blew out a breath, unhooked her seat belt and crawled over the console toward him.

His mind went absolutely blank, but his body knew what to do. It reached for her, hauling her into his arms and holding her tight. "You okay?"

"Peachy fine. Just trying to reassure you in case you're scared." One of her knees was dangerously close to unmanning him but when he went to shift her, she couldn't be budged.

"Are you?" she whispered. "Scared?"

"Terrified," he murmured, and she burrowed right in, curling into him, pressing her face to his throat as her arms snaked around his neck so tight he could scarcely breathe, and he didn't care. He ran his hands up and down her back until she lifted her face enough to bump noses with him.

He slid his hands into her hair to hold it back so that he could see into her face, but she wasn't freaking out as he'd thought. She was staring at him with an awareness that stirred his own, straddling him, her legs on the outside of his so that the core of her was pressed up against the part of him suddenly very happy with the arrangement.

"Jase," she whispered, and then swallowed, staring at his mouth, her breasts mashed into his chest, her fingers in his hair. "I want to…"

He stroked a loose strand of hair from her temple and dropped his gaze to her lips, which she licked. "Want to…what?" Drive him crazy? *Done.* Make him hard? *Also done.* Make him want things he had no business wanting? *Done and done.*

"Trade positions back," she said.

"Okay." He was hard as a rock, and he knew she felt it because her hips made the slightest motion, as if she couldn't help it.

"Jase?"

"Yeah?"

"You're…"

"Yeah. It happens when you— God," he expelled

when she shifted her hips again. "*That.* When you do that."

"I never used to turn you on in the old days."

"I was a teenager, the wind turned me on."

A snicker escaped her, revealing surprise and delight, which didn't help his situation any. She really hadn't known she could excite him, and God, the look on her face, as if she'd just discovered she'd held all the power...which of course, she did. He wanted her, God he did, but then what? It'd be amazing, and he'd want more. He'd want all the spare time they could manage until either he left, or she did, and then...then he'd hurt her. Because he was not long-term material, not in his current condition. "Lizzy—"

She did that thing with her hips again and he let out a helpless, low groan, gripping her still. "Okay, enough of that," he said a little thickly.

"Sorry."

But she didn't look it. He was strong, he reminded himself. Physically *and* mentally. He'd had to be. He was certainly strong enough to set her away and get them back on track, before either of them took this too far.

And yet when she rocked her hips one more time, her eyes filled with marvel, he let her. Let her slide over the part of him now fully erect and straining for attention.

Yeah, because as it turned out, he wasn't strong enough to push her away after all. No way in hell.

"Mmm," she whispered in his ear, just a soft murmur when he hugged her in, and he nearly melted. Her hood had fallen back, leaving her hair a little wild, and her poncho gaped enough that when she leaned forward he could see down the sweatshirt she wore beneath.

She had on a pink bra with a little red heart nestled between her breasts. A pink bra with a little heart that stole his. Ah, man. "Lizzy."

She bent her head, and the tip of her nose grazed his jaw. She inhaled deeply, as if she loved the scent of him, as if she couldn't get enough, and his hands tightened on her. Everything tightened.

"You smell good," she whispered so softly he could barely hear her. "How is it you smell so good?"

"I don't know, but we—" Another arch of those hips, and *God*. He turned his face into her, burying it in her hair, closing his eyes, his hands running up and down her slim spine. Then they slid lower, feeling the curve of her ass through the rain gear and the sweats, and he forgot that they weren't doing this— instead he wished like hell that they were back at his place, in his bed.

She pressed her lips to his throat, dragged them slowly upward, heading toward his ear, and his eyes actually rolled in the back of his head. "Okay, that's—"

She nibbled on his earlobe and he sucked in a hard breath. *Going to turn me on and upside down and inside out.* He dropped his head to her shoulder and gulped for air like a man going under, and while he was at it, he gave in to the temptation and squeezed her sweet ass. "I can't remember what I was going to say. Hell, I can hardly remember my name."

She laughed. "I have a confession."

Oh, Christ, no. Not a confession.

"In high school…" She cleared her husky throat. "You didn't know this, but I had a big-time crush on you."

He lifted his head and met her gaze, and realized she expected a response. "Yeah."

"Yeah?" she repeated. "You knew?"

"A little."

"Oh." Her smile froze, faltered. Her hips stopped their deliciously slow assault on his senses.

"Lizzy—"

She climbed over him to get back to her seat. "We should go."

"Did you want me to lie?"

"No." She closed her eyes. "No. Look, it was a long time ago. I had a helpless, hopeless crush on you and hid it by being rude."

"You were never rude."

"No? And apparently I didn't hide it, either." She put her hood back up, hiding. "Come on. Before it gets worse."

He was pretty sure she didn't mean the storm. "It was a weird time," he said.

"Really, Jason? Were you socially awkward and gawky and geeky? Oh, wait, that was me. You were beautiful and perfect and popular."

"And you were smart, so damn smart. No, dammit, listen." He took her shoulders so she'd look into his eyes. "You were different—"

She snorted her opinion of that and pushed away his hands. "Different. You mean, I had a good personality."

"You did." He laughed when she growled at him. "And I mean you were *good* different. Amazing different."

"Oh, come on. You only talked to me because I did your work for you."

"Do you have any idea how cool I thought that was, that you were willing to help me and not want anything from me at all? You didn't care what anyone else thought. You didn't add up your worth by who you were sleeping with—"

"I didn't sleep with *anyone*. Not in high school, which I suppose you also knew."

Not completely stupid, he kept his mouth shut.

"Oh, my God. You said I kissed fine!"

"Actually, I said you kissed like heaven." He still remembered that day; the hot bleachers, the oak tree…the sun shining down on her hair, her eyes wide on his as he'd lowered his mouth to hers. He remembered thinking, *Damn Paul was an idiot, don't you be, don't screw it up for her.* And then their lips had touched and he'd been unable to think at all.

After a glorious few tongue-tangling moments under that hot sun, she'd stepped back, licked her lips and politely thanked him.

Then asked him to show her the rest.

"What?" he'd asked stupidly.

"The rest," she'd repeated in a low whisper. "Show me the rest, more of…this."

More? When it'd already been so much deeper than anything he'd experienced? He wasn't equipped for it, and for the first time in his life, he'd walked away from a girl. Just run off. So dumb, and so unintentionally cruel. He'd hated himself for not trying to explain it to her, for letting her think he didn't want her. Later he'd tried, but she'd refused to talk about it, telling him that if he brought it up again, she'd kung fu him in the family jewels. He'd believed her. "I can't tell you how many times I wished I hadn't walked away that day—"

"You didn't walk, you ran. But I understood. You had girls vying to give you the best blow job, and there I was, Virgin Lizzy."

He choked out a laugh. "Vying to give me a blow job?"

"Yeah, they used to brag about it in P.E. class."

"Lizzy, no one in high school ever gave me a blow job."

She just looked at him.

"I never got past second base in high school. Well, one time I got my hands down Cindy Potter's pants, but she wouldn't put her hands down mine."

"Everyone said you were the best kisser in the entire senior class."

"I should have been, it's all I ever got to do. Look," he said, smile fading. "About that day—"

"Seriously. What did I tell you about that? I am not going to discuss it. I'll still kung fu your ass."

"About that day," he said firmly, even while shifting clear just in case. "I could have had you, we both know that, but you were too good for me, and I knew that, too."

She looked at him for a long beat. "Do you really expect me to believe that a teenage guy turned down sex because I was too good for him?"

As he had then, he felt raw and exposed in a way he rarely allowed himself. "I wanted you, Lizzy. I wanted you as badly as you wanted me. I was just afraid."

"Uh-huh. You were afraid of the mouse."

"You weren't a mouse. I was afraid of what you made me feel, even back then."

She clearly didn't believe him, and why should she? He looked out the windshield; the storm continued to batter the car with wind and rain and debris. Inside, he felt just as battered. He'd naively thought he'd sleep the day away, maybe see his brother, eat, watch a few games, anything except think about the pain beneath his breastbone, the one that had Matt's name all over it. Anything except *feel*.

Ironic, when all he'd done since Lizzy had shown up was feel. "Lizzy."

"Please drive." She put on her seat belt, looking pointedly ahead.

She wanted to ignore everything between them. Fine. Far be it for him to bash his head against the wall of her stubborn-ass determination and, telling himself that, he put the Jeep into gear.

6

LIZZY WAS GLAD for Jason's silence. But a mile down the road, he slowed to nearly a stop. In front of them, a fire engine blocked the road.

Lizzy knew most of the fire personnel in town from working at the hospital, and she was happy to see it was Sam and Eddie manning the roadblock. They stood in rain gear, looking as wet and miserable as she and Jason were.

Sam and Eddie were from Firehouse Number 34, her favorite because the crew that worked it were like family to her. She attended a monthly card game there with Eddie, and often won. As for Sam, she'd actually gone out with him twice. He was cute, sexy and funny, but she'd learned that he made a far better friend than a potential lover, a decision that had turned out to be the right one since he'd recently hooked up once more with his high school sweetheart, Sara.

The guys were both happy to see Jason, and the three of them spent a minute catching up. She heard the name Matt for the second time and wondered who that was.

"Where are you trying to get to?" Sam finally asked Lizzy.

"Third and Cove."

"Ah." He shook his head. "You can't get there from here. And, hey, you weren't at the game the other night."

"I picked up an extra shift. And we *have* to get to Third."

Sam cut his gaze to Jason and shook his head. "Glad you're back, man. Good to see you safe. But to stay that way, you have to stay off Third."

"It might be an emergency," Lizzy said.

"There's twenty-four inches of water running through downtown," Sam said. "We've got backup units coming from all over the state, but what we really need is for the storm to pass. I'm sorry, Lizzy, but Dustin would kill me if I let you risk your neck."

"Dustin isn't here."

Hearing her desperation, he reached for her hand, eyes warm on hers. "What's the matter? Tell me what's going on."

"Cece's renting one of the Third Avenue condos. I think she might still be there."

He hunkered over to get his face level to hers. "Are you sure? They were told to clear out."

"You know how stubborn she is, and she's pregnant. Nine months' pregnant."

Sam let out a low whistle through his teeth. "She's not answering her cell?"

"It's off. I'm thinking she's out of battery."

"Or she's evacuated and out of range," Eddie said. "The river's taken over Third Avenue."

"I know, but I have to get in there to make sure." She turned to Sam, the softer of the two. *"Please."*

He grimaced, torn. "Lizzy—"

"Look, I'll come right back out again, I promise. But if you don't let me in, I'll just go in on foot."

Not doubting her for a minute, Sam nodded reluctantly, but he held her gaze as he leaned in and pressed a warm, careless kiss on her lips. "You have my cell."

"Yes."

"Use it. If you find her or if you can't—either way I want to hear from you. Ten-four?"

"Ten-four."

They pulled away, Jason handling the road with much more confidence than she could have even faked. "You and Sam," he said. "A thing?"

She was surprised at the question, but she knew she'd given him the right to ask when she'd crawled into his lap and nearly eaten him up. "We went out twice."

"I got a fairly possessive, protective vibe back there from him."

"No, you didn't."

He laughed softly. "Lizzy, the last look he gave me said 'I don't care that you're Dustin's brother, if you hurt her, I'll beat the shit out of you.'"

She took in Jason's broad-as-a-mountain shoulders, the sinewy arms that she'd seen without a shirt, the six-pack abs. Sam was built, too, but Jason had an edge that said he'd been to the bowels of hell and fought his way out and had no problem doing it again. "You're not afraid of Sam."

"No. I like Sam. I'm just trying to figure out if you like Sam, too."

She'd had boyfriends. Lovers. Not all that many, and she'd never kept one for long because she'd always put Cece first, even when Cece hadn't needed to be put there, and yeah, so maybe she'd used her as a guard against getting hurt, but whatever. She'd still been with enough men to at least know her own needs. And right now that need was to remain single. Besides, she refused to take a giant step backward just because the guy of her early fantasies was sitting next to her, looking at her, rendering her a teenager again with one slant of those slate eyes.

He'd known about her crush.

That was bad enough. She had no intention of telling him she'd apparently never *stopped* crushing on him. "Sam and I are just friends. And there's no one else, either. I would never have kissed you the way I did if there was. I'm single if that's what you're asking, and I intend to stay that way."

He looked at her for a quick beat before turning back to the road. "Me, too. Look, to be honest, I'm damaged goods at best." Once again, he glanced over at her. "Screwed up in the head," he clarified. "It's not exactly conducive to a relationship."

"Does that have anything to do with Matt?"

"I guess it does."

"And he's…"

"Dead." His fingers tightened on the wheel. "And, Jesus, that never gets easier to say."

"A close friend?"

"The closest." His voice had lowered, and was laced with pain. "He died on a rescue mission in the Midwest floods six weeks ago." He eyed the flooding all around them. "Try to appreciate the irony. I certainly am."

"Oh, Jase." She understood the pain. "I'm so sorry. What happened?"

"We were there pulling people out of a building that had collapsed. I was in the rescue boat and Matt was in the water, trying to reach the victims. There was a hillside, creating a sort of waterfall. We were working not to go over while trying to get everyone in the boat." He was silent a minute. "Matt was shoving people up to me and I was lifting a badly injured kid when the boat got caught in the current and capsized. Matt was trapped beneath it, and drowned."

His voice broke a little on the word, and her heart broke for him. "Were you hurt?"

"Cracked a rib, concussion." He shrugged. It was nothing, the gesture said. Nothing compared to being dead.

"Shit. Hang on."

She turned forward and saw the problem—two

fallen power lines across the road, with the water rushing over and under them so that they writhed like snakes, and sparkled like fireworks.

Lizzy braced herself as Jason hit the brakes, but he handled the Jeep like he'd been born to it, and the vehicle came to a controlled stop right in front of the downed lines.

Staring through the howling winds and curtains of rain, he shook his head. "Not good."

"Should I call the PUD?"

"Definitely." He pulled out his cell and tossed it to her while he backed the Jeep up, away from the live wires. "I'm going to take a closer look."

Lizzy nodded as she called information, but when she could only get a recording at the Public Utilities Department, she hung up. The wind shook the Jeep, making it shudder. She looked out the windshield and literally saw nothing but gray as the air thickened with rain and God knows what else.

She could see no landmarks.

No Jason.

She opened the door and, squinting against the spray of rain, yelled, "Jason!"

Nothing.

She pictured him trying to move the line and getting electrocuted, and was about to run out into the storm when suddenly through the thick air she saw his outline.

Relieved, she pushed away from the Jeep, hands out until she slid her palms over his shoulders.

He turned to face her, his hands immediately reaching for her. "What are you doing?"

"Hoping you weren't electrocuted."

"Come on, back in the Jeep." Turning her away from him, he stayed steady and solid at her back as they staggered to the Jeep.

Inside, he sagged back and wiped the rain from his face. "Hoping I wasn't electrocuted," he repeated. "Jesus, I know how not to get electrocuted."

"It's so bad," she murmured, staring out the window. "So very bad. The whole day…"

"I don't know." He looked over at her, drenched to the skin, his lashes spiky black. "It's had some good moments if you ask me."

Something within her turned over. Her heart, she realized, exposing its tender, vulnerable underbelly.

"Tell me why you're not a doctor," he said quietly.

"What does it matter?"

"It matters to you, or it did. That was all you talked about, going to Los Angeles, being at UCLA, going through medical school so that you could be an E.R. doctor. Everyone knew how much it meant to you."

"It's complicated. My parents died. Two weeks after graduation."

"My God." He shoved his hair back from his face. "How did I not know that?" He just shook his head, clearly stunned. "You were so young."

"Older than you when you lost your dad."

"But I wasn't alone. I had my mom and Dustin and Shelly. Who did you two have?"

"No one, which is why I couldn't just go to L.A."

"So you stayed and gave up your dreams."

No. She'd never given up the dream. But after six months, she'd known she wouldn't be able to leave Santa Rey. Cece had been a lost, grief-stricken hell-on-wheels teenager. It'd taken a lot of attention and effort to keep her reined in, which meant she'd had little time for anything else.

But it'd been worth it. Cece *had* grown up and taken responsibility for herself. She was doing great, too, with the sole exception of having gotten pregnant by a complete asshole loser. "I'm good with how it all turned out," she told him quite honestly. She'd come to love her job, and would be sad to leave it. "And actually, I'm going in the fall. The hospital gave me a scholarship for medical school."

"I'm glad for that," Jason said quietly.

Yeah. Everyone was glad for that.

Except, oddly enough, her. She kept telling herself it was because it hadn't hit her yet, that's all. She'd be over the moon once she got started.

A heavy gust shook the Jeep. In front of them, the street was becoming lakefront property. She'd never seen anything like it, with the swirling sheets of rain, the shocking howl of the wind.

Complete havoc.

"So now I know how you got to be so tough," he

said, reaching over to lightly stroke a finger on her temple, pushing a wet strand of hair away. "So tough, and so unwilling to accept a hand. You lost your support system, and then had to become Cece's. You're used to counting only on yourself."

"Yes."

"Is it really so awful to let someone help you?"

"I'm letting *you* help," she pointed out. "Even when I know that this is all a moot point, that Cece is fine." She paused. "But I'm grateful."

"I don't want you to be grateful."

"What do you want?"

"So suspicious." He ran his thumb along her jaw, played with her earlobe. "Maybe I just want a peek at your sweet and sunny disposition."

She had to laugh at that, even as parts of her tingled. She wasn't sure what they were going to do with all this shimmering chemistry, but she had an idea, and it made her shiver. "Jason."

"Lizzy." He leaned in, his mouth nearly connecting with hers, letting the anticipation build for a beat, until—

Something smacked into the car hard enough to make her gasp and jump. It was a large branch, which rolled off the hood, landing in front of them. It caught on something in the water and snagged, blocking their way.

Jason looked out and shook his head. "I'll get it."

He'd just shut the door when his cell phone vibrated in her pocket. She'd forgotten she had it. She debated with herself for a minute, then flipped it open. "Jason's phone."

There was a moment of silence, then a soft, unsure female laugh. "Well, hello, strange woman answering my brother's phone."

Oh, boy. "Uh, hello. Hang on, I'll get him—"

"Oh, no, please don't. I'd much rather talk to you because Jason won't tell me a damn thing except that he's alive. Is he okay? Is he really okay?"

Lizzy took a peek at Jason as he came back into the Jeep. "He is."

"Is he exhausted?" his sister asked. "Pale? Are his eyes haunted like they get when he's first on leave? Because he says he's fine, but that's all he ever says since Matt. So maybe you'll tell me the truth. Is he still hurting?"

At the love and worry in her voice, Lizzy softened immediately. "Maybe a little."

Jason slid her a look. "Who is it?"

"Your sister."

"Don't tell him I'm drilling you!" Jason's sister whispered frantically. "He'll take the phone and tell me he's fine. That he's not still blaming himself for Matt's death."

Lizzy felt an overwhelming surge of emotion for his sister, and for Jason. It felt like protectiveness, empathy. Affection.

And more, so much more. She felt the need to

wrap herself around him and squeeze until he felt
better, or until *she* felt better, whichever didn't come
first—

"Listen," his sister said quickly. "Whoever you
are, promise you'll at least feed him. That you'll—"

Jason gently relieved Lizzy of the phone. "Shelly.
It's sort of a bad time. Can I call you back?" He listened to what sounded like a long litany and rubbed
a spot between his eyes. "Well, I *am* fine."

Lizzy had been looking at him all day, and yeah,
no doubt he *was* incredibly fine, but she could see
beneath the surface now, past the rugged face and
body *which* tended to rob her of cognitive thought,
and she agreed with his sister.

Beneath the easy, calm, I-can-handle-anything air
he wore, there *was* that edge she'd already seen, that
haunted hollowness she now understood. And added
to both was a sheer exhaustion that probably went to
the bone. As she'd worked all night, he wasn't alone
in that, but Jason was more than just physically tired,
and her heart ached for him.

"I promise," Jason said in the affectionate but frus-
trated voice that was a universal sibling-to-sibling
tone. "I'll come see you and Mom the second the
storm's over and I'm free." He looked at Lizzy. "I'll
invite her, yes, but the decision is hers." A reluctant,
fond smile curved his lips. "Yeah, you, too, brat.
Bye."

"They love you," Lizzy said softly into the silence.

Well, not silence. There was no silence, not with the whipping wind and rain hammering the poor Jeep.

"They love me," Jason agreed, craning his neck to look around them. "But love isn't going to get us out of this mess."

Water was rushing and running beneath the Jeep's tires, the force of the storm rocking them back and forth. No. Love wasn't going to help them. "I'm sorry. I can't believe I took us out in this."

"Don't be."

She knew Cece was capable, dammit, she knew. But a small part of her couldn't help but try to be there, just in case Cece still needed her.

Hell, maybe even a small part of her *wanted* Cece to still need her. "Aren't you glad you came home for some food and rest?" she asked drily. "And…what else was it you wanted?"

His eyes heated, and her breath caught. "Oh, that's right," she murmured. "Sex. You wanted sex." At just the words out of her own mouth, something deep inside her belly quivered. She peered out the window toward where she knew the power lines were. "And I nearly gave you electrocution. Man, did you get ripped off."

"Guess that means you owe me."

She turned back with amusement. "Is that right?"

He just smiled.

"Are you really suggesting I owe you sex?"

He arched a brow. "Is that on the table?"

"No. I was just wondering."

He laughed. "God." He swiped a hand down his face. "Somehow, even in the middle of hell, you can still make me laugh."

Lizzy took in his smile, and how good it looked on him, and smiled, too. "I really like this whole not being in awe of you thing."

"Well, damn. I am going to miss the awe."

Now *she* laughed. "Are you ready then?"

"For the sex?" he asked hopefully.

"Ha. No, but nice try." She grabbed her bag and tossed him his. "I assume we have to walk from here."

"There's no way to get the Jeep past the wires."

"Okay." She looked at her watch. Past noon already. Unbelievable.

"Wait," he said when she reached for the door handle. Leaning in, he pulled up her hood, his fingers warm and callused, the touch going right through all her protective layers and her inner brick wall, making itself at home right in the center of her heart.

"That's not going to help for long," she told him, her voice a little husky.

He kept his fingers on her, and lightly stroked her jaw. "Stay close. There'll be underwater currents, and if your feet get swept from under you—"

"I'll be okay. I *will*," she said with soft steel when he started to speak again.

"I know." He looked at her, then hauled her to him

and kissed her hard and long, with a promise of more to come. Then, still breathing hard, they opened their doors and headed out, meeting at the back of the vehicle. Jason grabbed her hand, and together they trudged for higher ground, with Lizzy hoping that Cece—in labor or not—had done the same.

7

DOUBLE FISTING her flashlight, Cece waddled down the flight of stairs to the single-car garage beneath her condo unit, where she made the unhappy realization that the entire place had sprung a leak.

There was four inches of water swirling at her feet.

Which was perfect, really, because now it was official. The day had gone to hell in a handbasket.

She surveyed her car, which was as useless as her phone, because the garage door was shut and she had no electricity to open it. In the corner, soaking up water, was a bag of skinny clothes, also useless.

And the raft from last summer's river trip…

No.

She couldn't.

For a moment, she stood there in indecision— never a good state for her because being indecisive made her do things without thinking.

Stupid things.

Like having sex without a condom.

Way late to rue that decision, she reminded herself.

Besides, she was getting a present out of the deal, the best present she'd ever had; she rubbed her belly. "Don't you worry, baby. You really are the best thing to ever happen to me."

In response, her stomach banded tightly.

Another contraction.

"Oh, God." She clutched the hood of her car for balance and breathed through it. Then when it passed, she waddled past the car, knowing there was a manual lever somewhere, which would allow her to open the garage door by hand. She was going to have to risk her bad tires, and drive herself to the hospital.

To reach the lever she had to stand on the bucket of Pretty-In-Pink paint she'd bought on sale last week. She didn't know if she was having a boy or girl, she'd refused to peek, but she was all for hoping. Buying the paint ahead of time was one thing—it'd been half off, and a deal she couldn't pass up. But actually painting the walls with the pink had seemed a little bit like taunting that bitch Karma. So she'd waited.

And now she was tempting Karma anyway. Gritting her teeth, she managed to climb up onto the bucket. Barely reaching the lever, she pulled. It was much harder than she expected, and she had to tug with all her might. As the garage door slowly lifted, she lumbered down off the bucket for better leverage, sweating in spite of the chilly wind and rain flying through the opening as it widened.

And that wasn't the only thing she could see as the door slowly rose.

She saw a pair of kick-ass motorcycle boots, topped by long, leanly muscled legs inside a set of jeans faded in all the stress points.

So not Lizzy.

As she gasped and backed up a step, another contraction hit, and her last thought as she sank to the ground was *shit*. Her worst nightmare was coming true—she was going to have this baby in front of a perfect stranger, and a bad boy to boot.

Just her luck.

JASON AND LIZZY SLOGGED their way along the streets toward Eastside. For now they were above the worst of the flooding, but she knew that at some point within the next half mile they'd have to turn and cut across the roads, heading down into the areas quickly filling up with runoff water from the hills.

They'd had to stop twice. Once to help a guy climb over a huge fallen pine tree to get out of his driveway, another to help two college students—one of whom had broken his leg—get back to the roadblock to where Sam and Eddie were.

Lizzy took a glance at Jason. In profile, with his hood up, backpack on, face set, he looked like a soldier. Unreadable. Impenetrable.

Unapproachable.

And yet he'd kissed her. Touched her. Talked to her.

He hadn't been unapproachable then, not when they'd opened up to each other, and not when she'd been in his lap, straddling him, his hands all over her.

She'd never considered herself a particularly sexual woman. She liked sex, even loved it occasionally, but it didn't happen all that often. Her fault, she knew. It was that whole rely-only-on-herself thing.

And yet from the moment she'd seen Jason again, she'd been thinking about it. It was getting uncomfortable, all the thinking, and when her cell phone rang, she pounced on it.

"Just me," Cristina said. "You find Cece?"

Lizzy exhaled. "No. We're still trying to get to her place."

"*We* as in you and Jason?"

"Yes."

"Ah. You jump his sexy bones yet?"

"Hey." She hurriedly turned down the volume on her phone. "Jesus, Cristina."

"Oh, come on. Take a look at him and tell me you haven't thought about it."

She craned her neck and took him in—tense and edgy, wet and hungry, exhausted.

And sexy as hell.

Yeah, she'd thought about it once or twice.

Or a hundred times.

"We're a little busy," she said instead.

"Who's too busy to think about sex?"

Lizzy rolled her eyes and closed her phone.

Jason raised a brow. "Who was that?"

"Nobody."

"Nobody made your face red?"

"I'm warm."

He gave her a "yeah, right" look, but let it go. "No cars, no people," he noted, looking around.

Lizzy took her mind off jumping his incredibly well put together bones and nodded. "Everyone's already gone."

"Which means…"

"Yeah." She sighed. "She probably is, too. I told you, this is just me being overprotective."

When a heavy gust blasted them, taking visibility back to zero, he turned them both into the dubious safety of a tall oak along the side of the road. Pressing her back to the trunk, he bowed his body to hers to catch the brunt of the wind and rain.

She held on to him, more out of pleasure and appreciation of that hard body pressing against hers than out of fear.

"It's getting worse," he said in her ear.

The storm? Yes. Her ridiculous reaction to him? Double yes. She nodded, her jaw brushing his, and he pulled back enough to look into her face. Lifting a hand, he ran a thumb over her jaw, clearly mistaking her discomfort over how much he excited her for her concern for her sister. "We'll find her. I promise."

"I don't need a promise from you."

"Humor me."

She had to work at not turning her face into his palm. "Why?"

A half smile curved his lips as he watched her mouth, making her feel he could read her mind. "Maybe because I want you to owe me."

She choked out a laugh as he'd meant her to, and they began moving again. She pulled out her cell phone as she'd been doing every few minutes. Still nothing.

"We're going to have to cross soon, if the flooding lets us. Don't worry. I pretty much majored in Stubborn-ism. You, I'm guessing, majored in Ornery-ness. You know what that means, right?"

"That we'd kill each other in the long run?"

He smiled. "Besides that. It means we're going to get there. We won't give up until we do."

She looked into his eyes, steely and determined, revealing that while his tone might be easygoing, he was anything but. "Ornery-ness?" she asked.

"Yes, but I realize that it takes one to know one." He smiled at her, drenched, tired and not leaving her side, and something about him continuously grabbed her by the throat, by the gut.

By the heart.

"Thank you," she whispered.

"What did I tell you about thanking me?" He reached for her hand and squeezed it as they walked. "Besides, I should be thanking you."

"Because you're here in the wind and rain and craziness instead of having all that sleep you wanted?"

His mouth quirked. "And the sex. Don't forget that. But I mean because today, with you, I feel…" He shook his head, searching for words. "Alive."

A ball of emotion stuck in her throat so that for a minute she couldn't speak. "Well, then, maybe it's you who owes me."

He smiled, a warm, real smile. "That works, too."

They came to an intersection. Below, they could see the high school sports field, and beyond that, a grove of trees, then the school itself, and about a half mile beyond that, Cece's condo complex.

The high school football and track fields were under water. It was hard to tell how much from here, which wasn't nearly as much of a problem as was the fact that the street that ran between the high school and hill had become a gushing river.

They stopped before it. "New plan," Jason said, staring at the water. "You give me the exact location of her condo and I'll go get her."

"While I…?"

"Wait here."

She looked up into his face. He wasn't kidding. He wore a fiercely intense expression, with absolutely no softness in sight. None. "I'm going with you, Jason."

He sighed. Swiped a hand down his face. "Yeah, I figured you'd say that." His jaw tightened as he surveyed the area. The school buildings looked to be under a foot of water, which was rising with shocking speed.

She thought of all the news footage she'd ever seen of floods, and how the water seemed to always be up to the rooflines.

That it could actually happen here boggled her mind.

"Okay, here's what's going to happen," he said calmly. "You're going to do everything I tell you. Everything, Lizzy, to the T."

"Okay."

"I mean it."

"I realize that." She looked at the river which had formerly been Third Avenue. "The water's only a foot or so, right? No swimming required."

"Hate to disagree, but six inches of moving water can carry you away if there's a current, and there does appear to be a good one."

"I won't slip. I might not swim like a fish but I have good balance and I'm in decent shape." She'd be in better shape if she liked exercising, but there was no need to point that out.

He was looking at her, his gray eyes revealing frustration, and fear.

For her.

In her world, she was the one in charge, the one with the answers, and all the worry and stress: at work, at home, everywhere. How long had it been since someone had acted with her safety and well-being in mind?

Long enough that she couldn't remember.

"That water is really moving," he said. "So we're going to walk a little farther down to find a better place to cross."

"If Cece's in labor—"

"She told you she wasn't. But even if that's changed, you've no doubt delivered babies, right? And so have I."

"You have?"

"Two of them, actually. One in Katrina, one in Puerto Rico. We'll figure it out, Lizzy."

His confidence was oddly compelling and, even better, contagious. Once again, they took each other's hand and kept moving.

A QUARTER OF A MILE LATER, Jason stopped Lizzy, his gut tightening hard. They stood at another intersection facing a waterfall caused by a dam of debris more than fifteen feet high, blocking the street. Water poured over the fallen trees, house pilings, furniture, and a myriad of other crud, rushing onto Third Avenue in a crazy whirlpool, making the current hard and fast.

Deadly.

In the Guards, when he protected and served, it was for strangers, not someone embedded into his heart.

And she was embedded, crazy as that was. Once upon a time, it'd taken his job to make him feel alive, and now it was Lizzy doing that—Lizzy who was now in danger.

"Oh my God," she murmured at his side, clearly shocked.

"Not here. We can't cross here. We keep going."

She didn't argue.

It was another half mile before the water slowed marginally. "Better," he said grimly, knowing it was only *slightly* better, that they'd still have to backtrack to get to the condos, but his concern was the fact that things were deteriorating across the board, and deteriorating fast. He looked at Lizzy and wished like hell she'd stayed in the Jeep.

"Don't even think it," she said. "I wouldn't have stayed."

"So you reading minds now?"

"Yeah, well." She grabbed his hand, put it over her heart and looked into his eyes. "You're pretty transparent at the moment. Listen to me, Jason. I'm not going to get hurt."

What about drown? Are you going to drown?

She eyed the water. "I can do this."

"Counting on it."

They waded in together, him using all of his will-power not to grab a hold of her and never let go. At his side, she sucked in a harsh breath but didn't complain. And it was that, he thought, that one thing among many which told him this was somehow going to be okay. She wasn't soft, except for where it counted. She was tough as hell, and also, incidentally, giving him a much needed kick in the ass.

Not to mention the heart.

Debris floated in the current around them. Wood, car parts, a whole variety of things, weaving and bobbing and threatening their safety. But they were managing, and doing okay, when suddenly Lizzy gasped and pointed.

Coming right at them was an old metal fishing boat, sans engine, looking as if it'd seen better days. Packed in it like sardines were four men, two women and several teens. Two of the men were rowing, with the guy in the back yelling directions. "Right, Lenny! Right! *Jesus, your other right!*" When he caught sight of Jason and Lizzy, he cupped his hands around his mouth and yelled, "You two need help?"

The small boat wasn't meant for more than two, three people max. It was straining, seeming wobbly and unsteady in the relatively shallow water. Even if they found Cece in her condo just down the street, there was no way they could fit a nine-months'-pregnant woman in that boat. "We're good," he told them, waving them on.

"It wasn't steady enough," he told a silent Lizzy. "If she's there, we'll find another way to get her out— Oh, shit." He lunged after the metal boat as it headed nose-first toward the huge steel traffic light on the corner. He could hear the shocked screams of some of the occupants, including the guy still yelling, "Right, Lenny! *Right—*"

But he couldn't catch it in time. The boat hit the pole and people went flying.

Jason shoved Lizzy the rest of the way across the street, then headed for the closest two splashes, managing to snag a woman in his right hand and a teenage boy in his left before they were washed downstream. "You okay?"

They both stood up, gasping and coughing but nodding. Jason waited until they had their feet beneath them to let go, then turned to the others.

The guy doing the yelling had caught the boat. Everyone else scrambled back into it, still griping at one another.

Jason helped them hold it steady while the woman and her son got back in. "Take it easy on the steering," he said.

"We will, thank you." The woman reached out to squeeze his hand. "You're an angel."

No. He wasn't. Because he didn't catch them all... And as he thought of Matt, and all the people he hadn't managed to save over the years, he locked eyes with Lizzy, who was holding on to a sidewalk parking post, watching him as if he was a superhero.

Too bad he was nothing close.

Yeah, he had training in survival and rescue, but that was pretty much his only claim to fame. The rest of life—the emotions, the heart, the real stuff...ever since Matt's death, it'd all eluded him.

Lizzy sent him a half smile, clearly worried, leaving him no doubt that she felt real affection for him. And when he touched and kissed her, that affection smoked and burst into a heat neither of them seemed able to resist. Just looking at her caught something deep in his chest.

Yeah. Most definitely feeling again, which was something he could think about later, after he'd figured out what the hell he was going to do with himself. Leave…or stay. Leaving was easy. But for the first time in recent memory he wanted to stay right where he was. Wanted to fit in right here….

He headed toward her and her expression warmed further, and hell if that didn't do something to his insides, as well, telling him that leaving might not be the easy thing after all. "You okay?"

"Yes, I— Jason, *watch out*—"

That's the last thing he heard before he was plowed over by something hard and unforgiving. Before he could process anything except maybe "fuck" and then "ouch," he was underwater and down for the count.

8

"Jason." Heart in her throat, Lizzy leaped into the water toward where the fishing boat had run him over. *"Jason!"*

The occupants of the boat were an elderly couple who had no more control of the vessel than they had of the weather. The woman was staring at the water where Jason had gone down. "Oh, dear!" she cried, slapping her hands to her cheeks.

Jason didn't surface. Lizzy swam like hell toward where she'd seen him go down.

"So sorry, honey. I can't seem to steer like I used to," the man called out, dropping his oar and leaning over the edge to look for Jason.

Which was little to no help as his boat kept floating away. "Do you see him?" he called back. "Anywhere?"

"No, I—"

Just then, Jason surged out of the water, shook his head and whipped around to look at the boat that had just hit him. "What the hell?"

"They can't steer like they used to," Lizzy repeated, swallowing her half-hysterical laugh as she grabbed him. *"Are you okay?"*

"I'm fine." His eyes narrowed on the boat as it continued its merry path down Third, mostly because neither of the occupants could stop it. "They're going to kill someone."

It hadn't been him. That's all Lizzy could think. It hadn't been him. "You're *not* okay." Her heart took a hard hit at the gash on his forehead. She slipped her arms around him to hold him upright, even though he was as steady as a rock. It was *her* legs shaking like a bowl of Jell-O. "Come on, come here."

They waded through the water to the far side of the street. On the corner was a park. Or had been. With the rain battering the virtual sea around them, they headed straight to what looked like a wooden lean-to.

It was really a playground set, half-covered by water. They sat on what turned out to be the middle level of the jungle gym, using it as a shelter to get out of the driving rain for a minute.

Lizzy looked around the three-foot-by-three-foot area. She'd give her last penny for a space heater and dry clothes.

"You must be cooked," Jason said. "No sleep last night, literally running in this storm all day…"

"I'm okay." She slipped her backpack off and opened it, pulling out her first-aid kit.

"I'm fine, Lizzy."

"I know it." She lifted the gauze she'd opened and

scooted closer. He was sitting, leaning against the back wall, one leg straight out in front of him, the other bent, his elbow propped on it, hand holding his head, eyes closed.

"Let me see," she said.

He dropped his hand and set his head back. She kneeled at his side and pressed the gauze to his cut, applying pressure to stop the bleeding.

He sucked in a breath but said nothing.

"I don't think you need stitches," she murmured.

"No, I don't."

She looked at his face. His eyes were still closed and he looked pale to her. A muscle in his jaw ticked, and her heart sank. He was in great pain. "Open your eyes."

He did, flashing the gray depths at her.

"Not concussed, I don't think," she decided, relieved to find his pupils normal and reactive. "But we should get an X-ray just in case."

"Your nurse is showing."

It wasn't pain getting to him, she realized. He was *pissed*, and she stared at him as it sank in. "You're upset that you got taken down by that boat."

"Hell, yeah. They were older than dirt and couldn't get out of their own way."

She let out a low laugh. "Big enough ego?"

He stared at her in disbelief. "Ego?"

"Yes. You're being such a…guy."

"News flash. I *am* a guy."

"Uh-huh. Look, I'm sure you've taken a hell of a

lot worse hits than this. I'm figuring if you're okay enough to be insulted, then you're okay enough to continue. So if you're done sulking, we should go."

He looked at her for a long moment. "Your bedside manner could use a little work."

"Oh, sorry." She let her smile slip out. "Would you like to be fawned over?"

"No. Hell, no." But he paused, and then looked at her curiously. "What would the fawning consist of?"

"Funny. Let's go, big guy. Oh, and it's two-one now."

"What?"

"Before we crossed the new river running down Third, we were even, one-one. I saved you, you saved me. But now we're two-one, big guy. *You* owe *me.*"

He narrowed his eyes, then hissed out a breath at the movement.

"Careful. You're still bleeding."

"Yeah, and how exactly did you save me this second time?"

"It's all in the gauze work." She cupped the back of his head and pressed on the gauze with her other hand. "Are you going to go all alpha on me and get upset that I'm winning?"

"I didn't realize we were keeping score." He turned his head a fraction and she watched his eyes go from alert and sharp to…heated?

She looked down and realized their positions— him sitting, her kneeling—left him at eye level with, not to mention less than an inch from, her breasts.

He licked his lower lip.

And just like that, her nipples hardened.

Not that he could see her reaction. She wore his thick sweatshirt and a rain poncho, and was soaked to the skin, but it didn't seem to matter.

Her breathing changed.

And so did his.

Trying to act normal when her body was so hyper aware of his that it was quivering, she pulled the gauze away from his cut, bent over the first-aid kit and located Steri-Strips, which she put on the gash. She worked in silence, and he didn't say a word until she'd finished and sat back on her heels to regard him.

He looked right back at her, then skimmed his hands up to her arms and tugged, and with a little gasp, she ended up in his lap. "Yeah, you're winning," he murmured silkily. "More than you bargained for." His gaze dropped to her mouth. He slid one arm around her waist; the other skimmed up her spine to the back of her head, cupping it, bringing her mouth to within a beat of his.

Her heart kicked.

"Once upon a time," he said quietly, "I didn't know what to do with the things you made me feel."

"You always knew what to do with all the other girls," she managed.

"Yeah, but if you'll remember, that was all show. I really was an idiot back then."

"Yes." Her lips quirked. "Though a really hot one."

He snorted, and spread his fingers wide on her back. "You're different now."

"Meaning I can talk to you without tripping over my tongue?"

"Uh-huh. You have a confidence." His fingers slid beneath the poncho and played with the hem on the sweatshirt, slipping beneath that, as well. "It's sexy as hell, Lizzy."

"It's fake."

He shook his head. "You're comfortable in your own skin. I bet you're a hell of a nurse." He ran those warm, work-calloused fingers over her bare back. "Do you love it?"

His fingers touching her? Yes. Yes, she did.

He was looking at her, waiting for her to speak, but it was tough to talk while he shifted his hand around to her front, those fingers now playing against the bare skin of her stomach. "Do I love my job?" she repeated shakily. "Yeah. I do. It grew on me."

"Well, it fits you. When I went into the military, I had no idea if it would fit me."

"It did. At least for the time you were there."

"Yeah." His other hand joined the fray, sliding up under the back of the sweatshirt, skimming her spine all the way to her nape and then back down, letting out a shaky breath as the tips of his fingers caught on her bra.

"It was a rough time for you back then," she said,

sounding shockingly normal for a woman who had a man's hands up her top. "You'd just lost your father. You were tired of football."

"You remember a lot about me."

Yes. She remembered everything about him, but because that would probably put her into stalker status, she just lifted a shoulder.

"You cared about me."

"Yes," she whispered.

His hand urged her forward some more, until she lost her balance and had to set her hands on his chest. He closed his eyes as if to savor the touch as he continued to play beneath her clothing. "God, you smell good."

"You can't smell me. I'm half-drowned and wearing too many layers."

"I'll give you the too many layers." He pressed his face to her hair. "But you do smell good." Hands tightening, he shifted, adjusting her so that she was straddling him.

"Jase—"

"Shh. Just for a minute." His mouth found the sweet spot beneath her ear, the one that was an instant turn-on switch for her, which she hadn't realized until just now. When his tongue touched her skin, she gasped, and with a low breath of appreciation for her response, he pulled a small patch of skin into his mouth and sucked, turning her gasp into a helpless moan.

"God. God, you're sweet." He palmed her thighs, urging them open a little more, pulling her flush against him so that she could find him, hard beneath his layers.

Her head fell back, her eyes closed, and when he rocked up, she moaned. Then he fisted his hand in her hair, tugged her mouth to his and kissed her, hard and deep, like he was dying for her.

Which was only fair, because she was dying for him.

Yesterday she hadn't thought about him in forever, and today she couldn't *stop* thinking about him. She cupped his face to hold it to hers, but he didn't seem to be in a hurry to go anywhere. Instead he let out a low, rough moan of pleasure that went straight through her. It was heaven.

He was heaven.

"Didn't expect that," he murmured after they pulled apart to breathe. He pressed his forehead to hers. "You?"

Was he kidding? She'd known for years that she'd melt into a boneless heap if he ever touched her. What she hadn't known was that the reality of kissing him would be so much better than the fantasy. And her fantasy had been pretty damn good. "After earlier? Yeah."

A corner of his mouth curved and flashed a dimple that went with the wicked light in his eyes. "I came home thinking I'd figure out what I should do with myself, and to maybe shut my damn brain off for a while. Mission accomplished, because when I look at you, it shuts right off."

She shook her head with a smile. "Is it coming to you? What you want to do with yourself?"

"I know what I want to do with you."

She laughed. "You know what I mean."

"Yeah." He looked around at the river running by them. "Stay or go… Do something because I think I should, or because I want to." He shook his head. "I thought I had it figured out, but I don't. I have nothing figured out at all."

She ran her fingers over the bandage on his temple, and his expression softened as he grabbed her hand.

"I came here feeling like the rug had just been pulled out from beneath me," he said. "Knowing damn well I wasn't in any shape to enter into any kind of a relationship. I didn't expect you, Lizzy." Letting go of her hand to cup the back of her head, he nuzzled at her throat.

Her eyes drifted shut as he slid his hands back beneath her clothing, making it all but impossible to breathe.

"I didn't expect you, either—" She broke off on a shuddering gasp when his hands slid up her ribs, his thumbs barely grazing the underside of her breasts. "We—" She had to swallow. "We should go."

"Rest a minute."

"I'm fine—" Another pass of those thumbs and her knees wobbled.

Which reminded her that she was straddling him, holding him down as she pressed on the impressive erection he had going between her thighs. With a strength she didn't know she had, she rose to her feet and held out a hand.

He took it and let her pull him up. "That's some control you have, Lizzy. Given I'm the soldier, it should have come from me."

"I have as much control as you."

"You're definitely the stronger of us, always have been."

"Stop it."

"I'm serious. Remember Carla Alvarez?"

Oh, yes, she remembered the beautiful Carla Alvarez. "You spent a month trying to convince her to go out with you?"

"Uh-huh. And you finally told me to stop trying so hard, to let someone else make the first move once in a while. Which worked, by the way. She was my homecoming date."

Yeah. Lizzy remembered. It'd driven her crazy. *She'd* wanted to make the move on him, but hadn't had the nerve. She watched him re-shoulder his backpack, thinking she had the nerve now. It'd come hard earned, but she had it. "Jase?"

"Yeah?"

She fisted her hands tight into his wet poncho.

"What—"

That was all he got out before she yanked him close and kissed him. Kissed him until they were both breathless, and then she shoved him away.

He staggered back a step and stared at her. "Not that I'm complaining, but what was that for?"

"I have no idea." But she did. She knew exactly.

She was over holding back in order to protect herself from hurt. Over setting aside things she wanted, things like her education and becoming a doctor, or taking an extra shift instead of a vacation in order to make sure Cece had what she needed.

Cece didn't need her anymore, and life was too short. She needed to live it. She was going to get what she'd always wanted, which right at that moment was him.

9

CECE GRABBED her stomach as another contraction took over, this one deeper and far more intense than the last, and when she opened her eyes again, breathing as if she'd just run a marathon, she realized she was on her knees, clutching her belly. Worse, her stranger had come right into her garage, crouched at her side, and was supporting her with an arm banded around her back.

"There you go," he said in a low, gruff voice that went with the badass boots and leather jacket, which he wore over a plain tee and torn jeans, all matching the tough expression on his face. "Keep breathing."

She'd planned on it, thank you very much, perfect stranger.

"How far apart are the contractions?" he asked.

She had no idea. "Oh, God," she gasped as another hit.

"Not far," he muttered, summing up the situation with one brief, unhappy glance.

She breathed through the worst of the pain, and then

managed to look at him. She couldn't see past the brim of his cowboy hat, which didn't help. "Who are you?"

"Hunter. Hunter Bryant. I live next door. Who are you?"

She narrowed her eyes, still breathing like a lunatic. "No one lives next door."

"I just moved in a few days ago."

Well, if that was true, he was gone every night, which made him exactly the kind of man she did not need right now.

"Listen, is there someone I can call for you? Because I'm not any good at this."

"I haven't seen you," she said stubbornly. "Oh, God. *Goddammit.*" The pain came hard and all-consuming, and *nothing* like menstrual pains, damn her *damn* doctor who'd said they would be. "Did I die?" she demanded, gripping the front of his jacket and fisting it tight. "Are you my frigging angel of death, Mr. Badass Biker Dude? Because first of all, the irony? Sucks. And second, I'm not ready to go. I have a baby coming and I'm all it has. Well, me and Lizzy, but she's bailed me out of every mess I've ever gotten myself into, so it's my turn to finally stand up and do this right. Do you hear me? I'm not going. I *refuse.*"

He got to his feet and pulled her to hers, slow and steady, carefully holding on to her. He had dark hair, dark eyes, darker stubble on a strong jaw, and a deep frown that left a groove in the center of his forehead.

He was no happier about this than she was.

"You didn't die," he said. "You're very alive, as evidenced by your pain."

"Okay, good point. Fine. I'm alive. *And kicking,*" she warned him, huffing for breath, using him to steady herself in spite of her misgivings, because she was shaking all over. "And you should know, I really can kick your ass, especially if you're here trying to loot the empty condos. My sister makes me do Tae Bo, and I can kick you to Timbuktu."

"Tae Bo is an exercise regime, not self-defense, and I came because I heard you scream." He sounded as if a woman screaming wasn't all that uncommon in his world. "Tell me your name," he said, a quiet demand.

"I didn't scream." But then another contraction hit and she gasped, and dammit, screamed a little. When it'd passed, she was left panting. "Okay, maybe I did."

He was completely supporting her now, and when she could, she forced herself to loosen the death grip she had on him, but he kept his on her. "I'm going to pick you up now, Jane Doe."

"Ha. And, no."

"Can you walk?"

"Also no."

He held out his leather-clad arms. With a sigh, she closed her eyes. "You're a badass. Your kind is why I'm in this mess. I gave you all up."

"Would it make you feel better to know I'm hardly

ever badass anymore? Just sometimes on the weekend?" He added a smile.

She didn't return it.

"I'm kidding," he said. "And I'm sorry to tell you,
but we have to get you out, regardless of what you
think of me."

"I weigh two tons."

"I don't know," he said as he scooped her up. "One
ton, maybe. Definitely not two."

Her gaze flew up to his. His dark eyes gave nothing away. He was sporting at least two days' of
growth on his lean jaw. He wasn't smiling, wasn't
looking particularly kind or gentle at all, which
actually was a good thing. If he'd been either, she
might have fallen completely apart. As it was, she
really did have to keep it together in case she still had
to kick his ass.

With her in his arms, he stepped out of the garage,
his boots sloshing through water. As her eyes ad-
justed to the daylight, she gasped.

The storm hadn't let up, and the street was flooding. Her savior was standing nearly knee-deep in
water. "Ohmigod."

He was leaning over her, trying to protect her from
the rain and wind as he walked. "It's going to be okay."

"How?"

He didn't answer, probably because he was saving
his energy for carrying her. She blinked through the
rain into his face. He was thirtyish, she guessed,

maybe even younger. He had a scar slashing through his left brow, and another on the outside of his eye.

Savior, or scary ax murderer? "How do you know it's going to be okay?" she demanded. "Tell me."

"I don't. I just don't want you to panic and have that baby right now."

"Oh." She let out a low laugh, shocking herself that she even could. "You're not supposed to tell me that part."

"Why not?"

"Because it's too honest. People don't like too honest."

"I do."

"Yeah, well, I guess I do, too— Hell. Oh, *hell*," she whimpered, and tried to curl in a ball as another contraction hit her with the same velocity as a freight train. "Oh, God. I am not going to have this baby right here, right now, not by myself!" As she twisted and writhed in his arms, she let the pain take her. She had no choice, it came in heavy, unrelenting waves.

Vaguely, from somewhere far outside her world of pain, she heard Hunter swear roughly, and then she lost herself for a moment. When she came out of it, he was stroking her hair from her face and murmuring, "Keep breathing, that's it."

She opened her eyes. She was in the backseat of a vehicle and her stranger was buckling her in. "The storm—" She gulped for air. "We'll float away."

"Don't worry, it's a Hummer," he said. "It's a

friend's. I'm repairing it for him. My Harley was out of the question."

"I want my sister."

"Where is she?"

"At the hospital, she's a nurse."

"Okay, Jane Doe, let's go."

She gripped his big, warm hand in hers before he could move away. "Don't worry? Was that another empty platitude so that I wouldn't panic and have this baby on you?"

A very slight smile tweaked the corner of his wide, firm mouth. "You shouldn't ask a question that you don't want the answer to."

"Oh, God." She closed her eyes and bit back the need to lose it. "I don't want you to deliver this baby."

"Baby, that makes two of us."

"You know what?" She shook her head. "I'm just not going to do this. I'm not going to be in labor. Mind over matter, and all that crap. Okay?"

"Works for me."

"It's nothing personal. I just don't want another man near my parts, not ever again—"

He laughed, then sucked it up when she glared at him. "I'm not kidding," she warned him. If she'd had the strength, she'd have grabbed him by the shirt again and snarled right up into his face. "You're not going anywhere near my—"

"*Agreed,*" he said quickly. "Do you want to call your sister, tell her I've got you and that we're coming?"

"Yes. My cell phone died, and she's probably worried—" She took the cell phone he offered, but she couldn't get service. Then another contraction hit and hit hard, making her drop the phone. "Oh, God, oh, God…"

Hunter squeezed her hands and stayed with her, right with her, looking completely unnerved but not leaving her.

Something tugged inside her at that and it wasn't the baby. "You don't have to do this," she whispered miserably. "I'd probably be running hard and fast if I were you."

"No, you wouldn't. And I won't, either. And that—" he offered her a very small, very short smile, but it was a real one "—wasn't an empty platitude."

She had no idea why she suddenly felt like crying, but she blinked it back. "Cece."

"What?"

"My name is Cece."

He smiled, and it was a stunner. "Well, then, Cece. Let's get you the hell out of here."

THE NEXT SEVERAL HOURS nearly killed Lizzy. They were stopped by a police unit in a boat and had to talk their way past the enforced evacuation. Then they helped a family of four get across Third. And another after that.

When they finally made it to Cece's condo, it was nearly dark. It'd taken all damn day to get there, and the place was empty. Lizzy knew this because she ran through the rooms until Jason caught her hand. Solemn and exhausted, he pulled her to him. "She's not here, Lizzy."

Right. Which meant that Cece *had* gotten out, and was somewhere safe. Which also meant that she had proof that Cece no longer needed her anymore, and Lizzy could finally have her own life, guilt-free.

Except…except maybe she'd really been free all this time and simply using Cece as an excuse, when it hadn't been Cece holding her back at all.

But her own fear.

Tugging free of Jason, she took the stairs to the second level and looked in Cece's bedroom for the third time. The bed was unmade, her cell phone plugged in to a charger on the nightstand, not charging because there was no electricity.

Jason came into the room behind her, quiet, a solid, comforting presence. "What are you thinking?"

"I'm thinking that maybe she's at the hospital, or my place."

Jason pulled out his cell phone. *"Shit."*

"Wet?"

"Wet and fried."

She whipped out hers. Wet, too, but somehow miraculously, still working. Of course she hadn't gone for a full-body dunk like Jason had. She called her house, but the landlines were still down. She called the hospital but the lines were busy. She tried Mike's cell, but her neighbor didn't pick up. Then she got Cristina, and found out that the E.R. was still turning people away. She tried the San Luis Obispo hospital next, but Cece wasn't listed as being there, so she shut the phone and shivered.

Jason's hands settled on her arms. "This isn't over. You just need some sleep—"

"Where is she?"

"Evacuated, at a shelter, is my guess," he said.

"Yeah. Which means she's alone and afraid. Cold and wet—" She broke off because her voice cracked, horrifying her.

"Ah, baby." He turned her to face him and stroked a hand over her hair. "You're so tired."

She was. So damn tired. And cold. She set her head down on his shoulder, just for a minute, because surely nothing really bad could happen while she was resting against his broad shoulder.

"You need out of your clothes," he said, running his hands up and down her spine.

She knew this. She was a nurse. She knew they both needed to be dry, needed, also, fuel for their bodies, and rest, if only for a few minutes.

Jason pulled off her rain poncho, then the sweatshirt beneath, leaving her in just the T-shirt he'd given her, which clung to her like she'd just competed at a wet T-shirt frat party. He crouched down to untie her soaked shoes, lifting each foot to pull them off, along with her socks while she stood there and shivered.

"With the power still out," he said. "There's no hot water. No dryer. We'll spread the clothes out and rest while they dry."

"I've seen the movies." She looked down at the top of his head. "You're going to strip me, then give me a line about hypothermia and use it to get me into bed."

Still crouched in front of her, he raised his head and flashed a set of teeth in the dimming light. "Damn, you're onto me."

His mouth was smiling, trying to make light of what wasn't a light situation at all, but his gaze didn't even make the attempt. His eyes were dark, bleak and full of concern.

For her.

Oh, damn. He was *still* her greatest fantasy. "You know, I've seen hypothermia in people who've been out in far less than we've been."

Straightening, he slid his hands up and down her arms. "Does this mean you *will* crawl into bed with me?"

"Maybe. For the greater good and all." She reached for his sweatshirt, lifting it past his mouth-watering abs, pushing the material up until he took over, tugging it off. Her breath caught at his bare torso, hard and rippled with sinew. "We need to follow the rules regarding hypothermia," she said softly, her fingers running over the tattoo along his biceps.

"Rules?" he asked a little unsteadily.

"You have to take off everything."

"Far be it for me to break the rules." Lending a helping hand, he made quick work of the T-shirt and tugged down her pants, leaving her in only her bra and panties as he kicked off his own shoes. "Christ, you are beautiful."

And with him looking at her like that, she felt it, but suddenly, without the clothes, she got even colder, and her shivering became violent and involuntary.

Jason saw the change and immediately the sense of play left his face. He pulled her to him. "Okay, now we're getting serious. Warming you up, and then sleep. Sleep before anything."

"I just don't think I can."

He scooped her up. "Sure you can. It'll be dark in a few minutes." He set her on the bed. "With the power out, it'll be pitch-black. We can't do anything more until daylight anyway." He yanked down the covers and nudged her onto the mattress.

"K-kay," she said through her chattering teeth. "But only for a few minutes."

"A few *hours*," he corrected, stripping off his pants, getting into the bed with her, tugging the blankets over both of them. Then he pulled her in, deliciously warm and strong. "Sleep," he commanded.

She opened her mouth to tell him she didn't follow orders, but he felt so toasty that she sighed instead, and snuggled in.

And, shockingly, slept.

10

CECE WAS DOING her damnedest to pretend she was anywhere else other than in the storm of the century, in the back of a stranger's Hummer.

In labor.

"On a beach," she muttered to herself. "In the South Pacific. It's hot and dry and there's a cute cabana boy serving me a fruity drink—"

She broke off at the choked laugh from the man in the driver's seat taking her through the craziness toward the hospital.

Hunter. He of the tall, dark and quietly strong persuasion, with the badass 'tude.

"I'm pretending I'm not here," she told him.

"Good. Keep pretending. And when this is over, I'll get you that fruity drink."

"No can do. I'm done with badasses. No offense intended."

"None taken."

"Oh, and on my beach, I'm not as fat as a whale. Just so you know."

He met her gaze in the rearview mirror. "Are you seriously comparing yourself to a whale?"

"Well, look at me."

"I am. I have been. I just see a pretty woman, scared half to death and trying to be strong."

Her breath caught. And then again as the familiar tightening began. "Oh, God. Oh, shit," she gasped as another contraction took her, tunneling to her very core. She tried to ride through the pain, but the storm swirling outside the windows scared her. *What if they couldn't get to the hospital?*

She could see Hunter's broad shoulders, flexing as he shifted the Hummer. They were wide shoulders, strong and capable. God, she hoped he was capable.

And, damn, but this contraction was different. Harder.

"Close your eyes," he directed from the front seat. "You're on that beach, Cece. You're warm. Hot even, in your favorite bathing suit. And your favorite people are with you. Who are your favorite people?"

She was writhing on the seat, dying, and he wanted her to discuss her favorite people. "Anyone not talking to me in the middle of a contraction."

"I'm trying to distract you."

"I'd rather you do something more useful—like have this baby for me."

"Yeah, no can do, sorry."

"No, *I'm* the sorry one. I'm sorry my parents died when I was a teen, which made me angry and stupid.

I'm sorry that all the men I wasted my time dating in that stupidity only wanted in my pants, and I let them because that's how I measured my worth—by how many men wanted me. I'm sorry you're just the poor schmuck who had the misfortune of finding the preggo chick. The really pissy preggo chick."

He said nothing to that and, into the awkward silence, as her contraction eased, she bit her lower lip and fought tears. God, she was so tired of herself. "I'm just sorry," she whispered.

"Contraction over?"

"Yes." She sighed. "And also the pity party for one, though I might backslide at the next contraction."

"Fair enough. And for what it's worth, anyone who doesn't value you is the stupid one."

She was quiet a moment. "You're different."

"I thought I was just another badass."

"Okay, I'm sorry about that, too. You look like my usual asshole type, but since you're still here, you're already so much more."

Their eyes met in the mirror again, and it was the oddest thing, but she couldn't look away. "You asked about my favorite people. It's my sister," she admitted, since he'd given her so much and she'd given him nothing but trouble. She gripped her belly and tried to rub out the pain. "Lizzy's all I have."

"What about the baby's father?"

"He's not interested in being a dad. Or a boyfriend. Or anything, not with me anyway."

Hunter didn't say anything for a long moment, and when he spoke, she got the impression it was difficult for him to speak evenly. "His loss then. Hang on." The Hummer jerked and spun, and she let out a surprised cry, bracing herself for a crash, but instead they came to a sudden, rather easy stop. "What is it? What happened?"

"Road's getting tough."

She had a feeling that was the understatement of the century, but another contraction hit, and it felt as if she was being ripped apart like a wishbone. She cried out, then screamed, and when she opened her eyes, Hunter was unhooking his seat belt.

"Road's washed out."

She stared into his face, panting. "Oh, God, oh, God, I'm going to have this baby in a Hummer."

He climbed into the backseat with her and reached for her hand. "I'll go for help."

"No! You can't leave me."

"Look, you don't want me to have to—" He shot a glance at her protruding belly, then just below, and she'd have sworn he actually blushed. "I'll run."

She might have laughed at the fact that he clearly didn't want to deliver her baby any more than she wanted him to, but panic had taken hold of her. Still, looking into his steady gaze, a resignation came over her, even a peace. "Hunter?"

He shifted closer, squishing his big body farther into the tiny floor space, pulling her in for a hug. "Yeah?"

She waited until he'd surrounded her with his arms, because she was a weak woman and his arms were so very comforting. "It's too late to run for help," she whispered, and, accepting that sometimes Karma had to have the last laugh—like putting her in this situation with him, a man who looked like her usual guy but wasn't anything even close—she buried her face into the crook of his neck and held on.

WHEN JASON WOKE UP, it was pitch-dark. He didn't need the light to appreciate several facts. One, that they hadn't found Cece meant she'd evacuated, which in turn meant he had no reason to immediately get out of bed.

And two…the warm, nearly naked woman sleeping in his arms. She was snuggled in against him, her back to his chest, legs entwined, her hands holding one of his between her breasts. His arm, the one she was using as a pillow, was numb, and if he wasn't mistaken, she might have even been drooling on his biceps. Smiling, he dipped his head to the crook of her neck.

Still asleep, she hummed in pleasure and wriggled her butt, which caused a predictable reaction in him.

"Mmm," she murmured in her sleep.

Yeah. Mmm. He loved how she made him feel, and he kissed the back of her neck, then an inch lower, making his way to her shoulder, nudging the covers out of the way as he went. She was hot, and sweet, and still sleepy enough to drop some of her guardedness. That, or somewhere along the way, through all of the crazy long hours they'd spent together, she'd come to trust him.

He'd take that, because for some reason, this woman mattered. Having her trust him mattered. He could hear the storm still beating the hell out of the building, but also knew there was nothing they could do about it, about anything, until daylight.

Right now, right here, it was just them. "Lizzy."

"Mmm," she said again with a soft sigh, still out cold.

He shifted to get even closer, and so did she, and her silk-covered breast filled his hand. Her nipple hardened through her bra against his palm, and she made that "mmm" again, and then—

Went utterly still.

"Jase?" she whispered.

There she was. "Expecting someone else?" He lightly sank his teeth into her shoulder, then kissed the spot.

"Oh, God."

He really hoped that was *oh, God, you feel so good* and not an *oh, God, this isn't happening,* but then she sat straight up, cracking him in the chin as she did.

"Ow," he said.

"Is it morning?"

"No. It's only…" He peered at his watch. "Two. Come here." Instead of waiting, he reached up, slid his arms around her sweet bod and tugged her back in.

"Oh," she breathed, rocking her ass into him, wrenching a groan from his chest. "We're not dressed."

"We are not," he said.

"The danger of hypothermia is gone," she whispered.

"Yes, since I'm hot as hell." He grazed his thumb over her nipple. "And, God, Lizzy, so are you. So damn hot."

She turned her head and peered through the dark up at him. She didn't shove him away or try to move. She reached up and touched his face, open to him in a way she hadn't shown before now.

Not realizing how much he'd needed that from her, he let out a breath and felt the last of his blood drain from his brain, heading south for the winter.

"We slept together," she murmured.

There was a blue glow to the night, washing over her face, casting them in contrasting shadows even as it highlighted the shine of her eyes, the curve of a breast, the arch of her hips. He skimmed his hand down her side, over her thigh and back up again, stopping short of her panties, letting just the tips of his fingers play beneath the silky material. He'd once felt things for her that he didn't understand. He still felt those things, only he understood them now, not that *that* made them any less terrifying. "Not *slept* slept."

"The rules of hyperthermia don't say anything about not having sex."

"No."

"I've always been one for following the rules." And she wriggled again.

He groaned, but no words came out of his mouth because, with no blood left in his brain, he couldn't talk. Could only feel as she pulled his head down to hers, her mouth sweet and eager.

God, he wanted this, wanted to connect as he hadn't managed to do all those years ago, as he hadn't managed to do at all lately because these days, thanks to his profession, his life was always on the edge.

No softness.

But here she was, warm and naked and very, very soft. It made him ache, ache to change the way he'd been dreading the future, ache to have hope instead. Hope that he could find peace, happiness.

Love.

It'd been a damn long time for him, and that it was Lizzy, the girl who'd once stolen his heart without even knowing it, made it all the sweeter. Lizzy all grown-up and dancing a hand down his thigh, squeezing the muscles there as she rocked that sweet ass into him.

She was killing him. Killing him. He unhooked her bra at the same time that he dipped his head and kissed her shoulder again, skimming his hand up to cup her now bare breasts.

A low, hungry sound escaped her as she clutched his wrist as if to hold his hand to her.

He didn't need the encouragement. Her breasts

were perfect handfuls and he could spend all day touching them.

"I've always wondered," she murmured.

"Wondered what?"

She hesitated. "If you're as good at the rest of this as you are at the kissing."

He huffed out a low laugh against her skin as he rasped his thumbs over her nipples, back and forth, making her stretch and let out a shuddery moan, shifting her hips restlessly. "I'll give it my best shot."

"Thank you—" She broke off with a soft gasp as he hooked a finger in the edge of her panties.

"I do my best work without these." He tugged them off, then slid a hand between her thighs, where he found her creamy wet and hot.

God, so hot.

He played there, his fingers gently opening her, finding what he sought, dragging a callused finger over slick flesh as he nibbled on her shoulder, the back of her neck, her ear…

"Okay," she managed. "You are good—" She let out a shuddery breath as he slid a finger into her. "Really good…"

"Shh." He had a plan. Tear at her defenses until she let him in. And maybe, just maybe, she'd do the same for him. To that end, he kissed her neck, and with every glide in and out of his finger, scraped his thumb over her center. She arched, holding him to her, and when her breathing changed into quick, desperate pants, he knew that she was close, so very close. As she tightened around him, he added another finger, and she burst with a soft cry, coming apart in his arms.

As she relaxed into the mattress, he nuzzled at her throat.

"More," she murmured. "The rest."

That worked for him. "I have a condom some-where gathering dust in my bag—"

"I'm on the pill." Turning her head, she blindly sought his mouth. "And it's been a long time for me. You?"

"*Very* long." Things got a little crazy then, as crazy as the storm wailing outside, and the next thing he knew, she'd rocked her hips back and he'd rocked forward, and he was inside her from behind, deep inside, surrounded by all that silky, wet heat. "God," he breathed with a shudder. "*God.* I've never—"

"Never?"

"I mean—not without a condom."

"Me, either," she whispered, and arching back, lifted an arm around his neck, gasping his name when he began to move, thrusting into her, slow and deep, speeding up as she shifted her hips to meet his, both of them breathing like lunatics. When she cried out his name, he nearly came from that alone.

It'd been so long.

So damn long, and she was doing as he'd known she would, slowly destroying him, tearing apart his defenses, letting herself inside his heart, making herself at home there.

And she had no idea…

"God, Jase…don't stop…" She was moving with him, letting out the sexiest little pants and whimpers he'd ever heard every time he pushed into her. When he slid his hand back between her legs again, she burst in a series of gorgeous tremors that took him with her straight over the edge, where only one coherent thought managed to stick.

Cast him a line, because he was going down.

11

CECE HAD TO GIVE Hunter credit—he was cool under pressure. He simply seemed to accept what fate had brought him that day—a hugely pregnant chick. One who was losing it.

"Oh, God," she whimpered. "Goddammit."

"Another one?"

"Another one, the same one." She tried to curl into a ball. "It's all the same one."

"Look at me. Cece, focus on me."

She inhaled sharply and, following his calm, assertive request, stared into his eyes.

It'd been hours. She hadn't let him go for help. He didn't have reception on his cell phone so no one was coming for them.

It was just the two of them, alone, in this together.

He'd told her that eventually, probably at first light, the emergency crews would make a sweep and find them. It'd been her plan to wait for them.

She'd hoped that was still a viable plan, but she sincerely doubted it because this baby was coming—soon. She knew it.

And so did Hunter.

"How are you doing?" he asked, stroking her hair back.

"I'm losing it, big-time."

"You're not."

There was admiration in his voice, which she marveled at. She'd told him about herself, practically thrown her past at him, and he still was looking at her as if she mattered. "Tell me about you," she whispered. "Tell me your story."

"You have other things on your plate right now."

She managed a laugh. "But we're about to get fairly, horrifyingly intimate here. As in I'm going to drop a baby into your hands. I could use a little distraction."

"All right. I work at the nine-one-one dispatch center for the county. I'm the night dispatch supervisor there, that's why you haven't seen me. I moved from Texas to take the job because I wanted a change."

"Change as in you cheated on your wife and she kicked you out?" she asked, fishing.

His mouth quirked. "No. There's no wife."

"Okay…change as in your girlfriend wanted a diamond and you bought a Harley instead and ran off?"

"No girlfriend, either, not at the moment. And my Harley's ten years old and paid for. If I wanted to buy a diamond ring, I would."

She stared up into his calm, very pleasing-on-the-eyes face. "I know you have baggage. Everyone has baggage. I need to know yours, Hunter. Start with your family. Truth. Are they crazy?"

"No." He smiled again, and she decided she loved it when he smiled. "Well, maybe a little," he corrected. "I have five older sisters, three brother-in-laws, two elderly parents, and let's see…*seven* nieces and nephews. All is good there, sorry to disappoint you."

"What about crazy exes? You can tell me—you're a serial dater, right? Love 'em and leave 'em?"

"I've had several long-term relationships, but they ran their course."

"Okay," she said, talking fast because she wanted to get to this before her next contraction, needed to get to this. "Maybe you're not hearing me. I'm going to need a flaw here, a biggie, Hunter. Preferably *before* I take off my panties for you."

"What?"

"Hello, *baby coming*."

He let out a shaky breath. "Right. A flaw…"

"Quick," she gasped as the next contraction took her and the first urge to push came. "Oh, God. That's not quick, Hunter!"

"I'm stubborn," he said quickly. "Completely mule-headed if I think I'm right. I can be a complete ass."

"Yeah? Do you throw things? Hit people?"

"God, no."

"Then it's not a fault. Jesus, I'm about to pass the equivalent of a football out my hoo-ha, *think!*"

"All right." He clearly racked his brain. "I know. I like my forty-two-inch plasma more than I like half my co-workers."

She laughed. "Okay, that's a start. What else?"

"I'm a slob. I don't do my laundry until I'm completely out of clothes, and even then I'm likely to just go buy more."

"Serious?"

"Serious. And I don't own dishes. I won't wash them. My last girlfriend dumped my sorry ass because we tried living together. She made it one week and gave up on me. There. My deepest fault, exposed." He spread his arms. "I'm not live-in material."

She looked up into the steady gaze of the man kneeling at her side in the backseat of a Hummer, desperately trying to distract her, trying to keep her calm. The man who maybe was a badass, but at least he'd stepped up to the plate when she'd needed him, which was more than any other guy had ever done. "Her loss," she whispered, mirroring his words back at him.

IT WAS SO BLACK THAT Lizzy could see nothing, not what time it was, not what she wore—which was nothing—and not what Jason was doing to her.

But, Lord almighty, could she feel. And what she felt was his hands on her in the dark bedroom, turning her to face him, pressing her to her back. He held her wrists, anchoring them on either side of her head as his mouth came down on hers in a soul-destroying kiss. Then, when she was breathless, heart and all the good parts revved, he slipped down her body, kissing a breast, then sucking the hardened tip into his mouth until she arched up for more.

Working his way down, he stroked his tongue over her ribs, her belly, swirled it into her belly button, and then nudged her legs open enough for his broad shoulders, where he proceeded to drive her right out of her ever-loving mind with a fierce intensity that left her sobbing for breath.

Before she recovered, he surged up and sank into her, burying himself deep, and just like that, she found herself hovering on the edge again.

Without even the faint slash of a streetlamp or moon, there was nothing but sensation, sensation as she'd never known. There in the dark, he pushed into her again and again, and she wrapped her legs around his waist, wanting it to never end. He whispered her name, touching her everywhere, his hands warm and sure, his mouth hot and talented, as he slowly, languidly moved inside her.

God. God, she could hardly stand it, and she slid her fingers up his hot, damp torso to fist them in his hair, dragging his mouth back to hers. She couldn't see the flex and give of his muscles, but she could feel them, and she rocked up to meet him, feeling her toes curl at the wave after wave of pleasure crashing over her.

His hands slid up her throat to cup her face, their mouths only a fraction apart as she breathed out and he breathed in. It was shockingly intimate, erotic, sharing air as his body took hers higher than she'd ever been, straight to heaven.

She was going to come, come with his rock solid body buried deep in hers. He was close, too, she could hear it in his breathing, in the way he gripped her, in how his mouth opened on her shoulder. "Lizzy," he murmured, and that was it, that was all she needed, the sound of her name on his lips, and her release rocked her.

Her pleasure triggered his, and afterward, they remained entangled like that, her swamped with emotions and the feel of his body covering hers, a part of her wishing they never had to move, because she didn't want it to end.

"WHAT TIME IS IT?" she asked, slipping out of the bed, wrapping herself in the blanket to hold in his body heat.

He rolled over, and she looked back to see the glow from his watch as he brought it up to his face and blinked at it. "Almost five." His voice was low and husky.

Sleepy.

Sexy.

God, so sexy. And everything he'd done to her in the deep, dark hours of the night came flying back, making her face heat and her good parts quiver.

She'd actually forgotten how much she liked sex. Hard to believe, and she had a feeling she wouldn't be so lucky as to forget again anytime soon. "I want to go by my place."

Even as she said it, dawn was breaking through the black night. One peek out the window told her nothing much had changed in terms of the weather, and she looked back at the bed.

As naked as she, Jason had rolled over again, the sheets snagged beneath him, leaving him sprawled on his back, arms and legs going taut as he stretched.

Just looking at him caused a little catch somewhere deep inside her. Hard and lean and tough, and then there were the tattoos.

And those abs.

And those long legs.

And what he had between them…

No doubt, he was rangy and built and gorgeous. And for one glorious night, he'd been hers. She could wish for more, but that was a waste of time.

She was finally free of the day-to-day grind of caring for someone, fully free to do something important to her for a long time. She owed it to herself to follow through.

Even if a very tiny part of her was no longer sure that was still her dream.

God. She just wanted to shove all that aside right now and climb back in bed. On top of Jason. She wanted to have her merry way with that body.

Again.

All day long.

He propped his head up on his hand and regarded her in the barely there light. "You look so pretty standing there, Lizzy. Pretty and cold. Come here, let me warm you up."

She knew what she looked like in the morning. Bed-head hair. Pale face, probably lined from where she'd smashed it into her pillow as she tended to do. "I want to go."

"I know. Come here first."

He held out a hand to go with the request, and she stared at it. Big and callused, that hand had stroked and touched and revered every inch of her body, and just looking at it made her knees wobble.

Who'd have thought such a big, work-roughened hand could bring such pleasure? "Jase."

He simply wriggled his fingers and waited patiently.

So damn patiently.

She had no idea what it was about him that had her feet taking her back to the bed until her knees touched the mattress.

Smiling up into her face, he reached out and wrapped his fingers in the blanket.

And tugged.

With a gasp she fell over him, minus the blanket, which he tossed aside. With an appreciative growl for what he'd unwrapped, he tucked her beneath him and rolled on top of her, pinning her to the bed. "Better," he murmured, dipping his head to the spot on her throat that always drove her crazy. "You taste good."

"We—" She broke off as his hand swept up her thigh, over her belly, her ribs, to cup a breast. "Have to—"

His thumb brushed over her nipple.

She licked her lips and closed her eyes, arching up into him. "Go."

He bent his head and replaced his thumb with his tongue, making her gasp and arch up again. "Just want one more taste…"

When she was wriggling, panting, he kissed his way down her belly, pressed open her legs and kissed an inner thigh.

"Jase—"

The single word ended on a rough exhalation as he took his "one more taste," and then, holding her thighs open with his warm palms, took another.

And another.

"Jason."

"Love the way you say my name," he said against her, and then he sighed, licked her one more time, and came up on his knees, pulling her to hers.

She was shuddering, quivering, and she stared at him as he rolled off the bed. "You—we—I…"

"I know." He looked at her, his hair wild, his eyes hot. "We'll finish later."

Okay. Except that hadn't been what she'd been about to say. She'd been trying to say how mind-

boggling it was that he could make her feel so beautiful, so turned-on, so blown away, without even trying.

She'd been about to say how unnerving it was to
find herself realizing how much more than just a
crush this was.

But some things, she realized, were better left unsaid.

12

JASON CLIMBED up the stairs from the garage level of Cece's condo, and into the kitchen. Wet to his thighs, he pulled a river raft behind him, with two life vests in it. He had a lot on his mind, and not the least was that he'd just had the hottest night of his life.

He wasn't exactly sure what that meant except it couldn't be good news that he was goners over one soft, beautiful, tough-as-nails Lizzy Mann.

She stood there, looking at him, and his heart gave one good, hard knock against his ribs. He'd spent twenty-four hours with her, an intensely concentrated twenty-four hours, during which time he'd seen her run the gamut of emotions, and face things most people never had to face.

She was solid. Loyal. Smart.

Yeah, *goners* was a good word to describe his current condition. A smarter man might have seen this coming, from the moment he'd caught sight of those slay-me eyes. He should have run hard and fast.

Instead, here he was, wrapped around her pinkie, willing to do anything for her.

Which meant he wasn't just goners, he was screwed a hundred ways to Sunday.

LIZZY STARED at Jason as he came close, dripping everywhere. Her clothes weren't quite dry yet and they certainly weren't as warm and toasty as Jason's arms and body had been all night, but they'd do. With no hot water and no electricity, the morning routine had been simple. She'd "borrowed" Cece's extra toothbrush—which Jason had been kind enough to let her use first—and pulled on her slightly damp clothes.

"Found our way out of here," Jason said.

She looked at the raft, then into Jason's eyes and let out a breath. "Oh, boy."

"Don't worry." He set down the raft and came closer still, pulling her up to her toes to give her a warm, hard kiss. She couldn't tell him that it wasn't their mode of transportation that had worried her.

"Find any food?" Jason asked, setting her down, turning to the cabinets.

"A single-track mind," she said.

"Nope. It's a double track." Over his shoulder, he wriggled an eyebrow in her direction, telling her without words what else he could think about.

Impossibly, her lips twitched. "I found some snacks."

"Great." He looked around hopefully. "Where?"

They'd had sex.

That thought kept bumping around in her brain, which meant *she* was the one with the single-track mind. And it'd felt like a hell of a lot more than just sex. They'd connected more than just the required body parts, far more. Truth was, he'd made love to her, and now she felt all soft and dreamy and mushy, and that couldn't be good. She didn't work well with soft and dreamy and mushy.

"It's actually warmer out there than it was yesterday," Jason said. "Which doesn't bode well. Warmer air usually means more rain."

"Yeah." She'd looked out the window. The rain was still coming down. They were past the twenty-four-inch mark and climbing, and no end was in sight. The winds were still a problem, keeping the power lines down and unsafe. But flooding was the biggest concern. The street outside was nothing but a raging river now, which had overtaken the yards and the bottom floors of every building along it.

Cece's garage had over four feet of water in it and the level was rising. She'd never seen anything like it except for on the news.

But Jason had. He'd lived it, and it'd cost him dearly. "Here's what I've got." She revealed the Cheez Whiz and crackers in Cece's pantry and made him laugh. "I know, my sister has the palette of a puppy, or a twelve-year-old boy."

"Not seeing the problem," he said, already plowing his way through the crackers.

"I'm assuming you usually eat more healthy than this."

"I eat in bigger quantities, that's for sure." He stuffed a loaded cracker into her mouth, then opened the cupboard behind her.

She took in his long, lean, tough body. "So how do you keep in such good shape?"

He slid her an amused look, then abandoned his search, hooked an arm around her neck and hauled her in. "Well…I did just burn off a good amount of calories."

"Yes. Yes, you did." She felt her cheeks heat. "That was, um…"

His eyes were hot. "Fun?"

"Very. And…"

He arched an eyebrow.

"Good." And amazing. And brain-cell destroying. And off the charts… "*Very* good."

His smile was slow and wickedly sweet, and also wickedly naughty as he backed her up until the wall hit her back. Plastering a hand on either side of her face, he dipped down so that they were at the same eye level. "And that wasn't even my best work."

She was turned on and turned upside down by him, but it was so much more than that. He made her laugh, which was possibly the most attractive thing of all. "No?"

"Definitely not." He kissed her jaw and made his way up to her ear, which he gently sucked into his mouth, making her eyes cross. "I'm starving and tired," he murmured. "But when this is all over and we've slept for about two straight days?" He laughed low and sexy in his throat. "I'll show you what I've got."

The thought made her knees wobble. "When this is over, I'll be busy at work."

"Twenty-four seven?"

She pulled back and met his gaze, which was steady and sure. He was always steady and sure, she knew. *Always.* "Not twenty-four seven, no."

"So maybe you'll find a few hours here and there for me."

"Is that all you need, Jase? A few hours?"

"Hell, Lizzy…" He ran a hand down her body, squeezing her hip, flashing a little smile. "I don't know what I'm doing or where I'm going, but I'll take whatever time there is until I figure it out."

"In bed?"

He laughed again, softly against her skin. "Now you're just teasing me."

The idea of staying in his bed until further notice was intriguing and bone melting, but she knew herself. She knew how she felt about him after only one day. After a few weeks, or whatever he had, she'd have given him her body and heart in unison, and it would kill her. "I want to get moving."

"I take it that's a no."

"Jase." She sighed. "It has to be."

"So last night didn't do anything for you then?"

She thought of how many times he'd made her

come, and felt her body respond to just the memory. "There's more than just sex."

"Are you dumping me, Lizzy?" he asked softly.

Her heart caught. "Well, it is my turn."

"I never dumped you."

"Rejected me, then."

"And I most definitely never rejected you."

"Ran scared," she amended.

"Now that…" He leaned in for another kiss. "That's the honest truth." He rubbed his lips over hers. "Luckily, I don't run scared anymore. From anything."

"No?" She put her hand to his chest to hold him off. And to touch him. God, she was so mixed up. "Well, apparently that's my thing now."

His eyes lifted from her mouth and met hers. "So you really are going to run scared."

His tone suggested the ridiculousness of that, but it didn't make it not true. She *was* afraid, afraid of getting hurt. "Maybe I'm running scared of your eating habits."

Letting her get away with that, he turned back for a deeper foray into the cupboards and she let out a breath. When he came up with a can of ravioli, she shook her head.

"Trust me," he said. "I've eaten a lot worse for breakfast."

She supposed he had and, looking into his face, which happened to take her breath, she found herself once again marveling at the man he'd become.

"I want to see where this takes us, Lizzy," he said, finding a can opener and two spoons.

"Hopefully straight to Cece."

"Not the raft," he said, handing her a spoon. "You and me. I want to see this thing through."

"Where it's going to go is you going back to your job, and me to mine."

"So black and white, then. No gray?" He fed himself a big bite of cold ravioli, and then her.

She chewed it down and shuddered. "Not when it comes to playing with my emotions."

His smile faded. "You think I'd play with your emotions?"

"Not on purpose, no."

He stared at her, then released a low breath. "Okay, so you really let them pull a number on you."

"Who?"

"Everyone and anyone who's gone in and out of your life without care. Pick one."

"You don't know what you're talking about."

"Really? So you're not this careful and guarded because you've never been hurt? Because you don't feel you can trust anyone?"

"No. Absolutely not."

"Your parents left you."

"They died!"

"Still hurts," he said very quietly. "Still sucks. And they died, leaving a kid to raise a kid."

"I was an adult."

"Barely."

"Jesus, what's the matter with you?" She stared at him, then turned her back, hugging herself. "I said we're done and you have to psychoanalyze it? You've never been turned down for a second date?"

"Technically, we didn't have a first date," he pointed out, pulling her back around to face him. "Your sister is in constant-need mode, so you can't count on her. Who do you lean on, Lizzy?"

She told herself she didn't understand where this was going, even as the anger welled up and nearly choked her. "You really don't know what you're talking about."

"No?"

"No."

"So you don't use your fierce independence to sabotage your own happiness at every turn?" he asked. "You like counting on only yourself?"

"It's worked for me, all right?" She hugged herself tight, unhappy that she'd ever opened up to him. "And I have no idea what the hell you're talking about. We slept together for one night. It was practically an accident."

He raised a brow. "So you accidentally came three times?"

She struggled for words as she felt the heat flood her face. "We're only here, together, because I needed a ride."

"Lame, Lizzy."

Yeah, it was. And a cheap shot. "Okay, so I needed more than a Jeep, and you've been…helpful."

"Helpful."

"Indispensable," she corrected. "But regardless of what comes next, there's no future between us."

In the thick silence that fell after that statement, they pulled on the rest of their rain gear and went outside, not touching, not talking.

Third Avenue was nearly unrecognizable, thanks to the raging river flowing down it. The rain pounded the raft and the water around them, making it sound like they were in a rain forest. There were no cars, no people, nothing but Mother Nature still on her tirade.

"You think Cece's at your place?" Jason finally asked.

"I just don't know why she hasn't called." And that was the rub, the crux, the basis for the knot of worry in Lizzy's throat. If Cece had gotten out, if she'd gotten somewhere safe, she would have called by now.

Leaving Lizzy unable to help but picture her in labor somewhere, possibly alone, without a cell phone.

God. She could hardly bear the thought, and just as the burning in her throat threatened to overwhelm her, Jason reached out and took her hand.

She met his steadfast regard and felt his fingers gently squeeze hers.

She'd hurt him, on purpose, to make sure he kept

his distance—that she kept her distance—and yet he was still here.

For her.

And she had to wonder, if under different circumstances, they could have made this thing work.

13

"THE BABY IS GOING to come." Cece felt her panic bubble as she looked into Hunter's eyes, a man she'd known only for one day. "Oh, God."

"Okay." He said this utterly calmly. He'd held her hand and stroked her forehead for hours, throughout the entire night and morning. By some miracle, the water hadn't risen any more around them.

With dawn here, it wouldn't be long before they were found, but it wasn't going to happen in time.

"It's getting light," he said. "I can walk out—"

"Swim. You mean, you'd have to *swim* out."

"Whatever it takes. I can get you help now—"

"No. No, you can't. Please don't leave me."

He stroked her hair from her face. "I'd be right back, I promise. Cece, you might need more help than I can give you—"

"But the baby is coming."

"I know, which is why I—"

"No, you don't understand." She dug her fingers into his jacket and tugged hard, yanking him down her level. "You have to get down there and catch the baby."

He covered her hands with his, his grip firm and soothing. "Okay. Okay, baby, don't you worry about my part, my part's easy."

"Easy." She choked out a laugh. "We haven't even slept together and you're going to have to—"

"Look, it's still pretty dark. I won't be able to see much."

"Oh, God." She lay back and stared at the roof of the Hummer. "I can't believe this is happening. I can't believe I finally turned my life around, that I finally met a really great guy, and now…*this*."

"You don't have to tell him," Hunter said quietly. "You don't have to tell him about me."

She blinked through the haze of pain and felt another laugh ripple through her. "I meant *you*, Hunter. You're the really great guy I finally met."

"Oh." He looked at her, then let out a slow smile that changed his usually solemn, quiet face. Transformed it. "I thought I was just one of those assholes."

"I was wrong. So wrong— Oh, God." Gasping as the contraction slammed her, she tried desperately to ride the wave of pain, but she was tired of riding. Tired of pain. So damn tired. *"Hunter!"*

"Right here."

He was. He was right there. Which was more than she could say for any other man in her life, ever. "I really don't think I can do this."

"Sure you can." He continued to stroke her hair

back from her face and smiled into her eyes. "You're almost there—"

"No, I changed my mind. I don't want to do this anymore." She knew she was just babbling, half-delirious, making no sense. "Tomorrow would be better."

He shook his head with regret. "I don't think you have that option, Cece."

"No, seriously—" She broke off on a thin wail as the insidious, all-consuming pain completely took her. It felt like it lasted forever, but finally, when she could breathe again, she closed her eyes and lay back, panting. "I'm done. Cooked. Finished. I want to go home."

"Soon," he promised. "Soon, I'll take you wherever you want to go."

"Oh, God. I really have to push. You're going to have to—"

"I know." He ran his hand over her leg as he slid down to a better position. "It's going to be okay, Cece. It's all going to be okay."

"How?" she whispered miserably. "It's never been okay." She knew she sounded like a child, but at the moment, facing what she was facing, she felt like one. "I'm going to be a mom, Hunter. I'm going to be someone's mom, and I don't know how."

"It'll come."

"Are you kidding? I can barely control myself. I mean, I gave up looking for trouble, I did, but sometimes I have the feeling it's looking for me, you know? And no matter what I do, it'll find me." She squeezed her eyes shut.

"I do know. Look at me, Cece." When she did, she could see it in his eyes, that he really got it. Got her. "You asked for my dirty laundry, and I was flippant. I used to be one of those assholes you gave up. But I've changed. So have you. We can do anything now, including this."

"Trust me, I can't. In fact, I'm not going to. I'm not." She shook her head wildly. "I'm just not going to do it."

"Okay, listen to me." He was on his knees, between hers, looking fiercely into her face, his hands on her hips as he leaned in. "Turning your life around is more than half the battle, I *promise* you. Everything that comes after that decision is icing, baby, all icing. As for not knowing how to be a mom, are you kidding me? You have all that life experience. You'll know exactly what to do. All that's left is believing in yourself."

She felt her throat close up a little, blocked by emotion. "I'm not sure I'm that evolved."

"Fine. Then I'll believe for you. How's that? I'll believe in you enough for the both of us."

"Why?" she whispered, feeling something well up from within, something that felt alien but not unpleasant.

Hope.

Such painful, delicious hope. "Why would you do that for me?"

He smiled, and it took her heart. "Because everyone deserves a second chance. I got mine, and I want you to have yours. I've watched you struggle with the pain for hours now without giving up, Cece. You've talked about your sister being a hero, but, Cece, I think it's you. *You're* the hero."

Oh, God, she wanted to believe. "Are you sure?" she whispered.

"*So* sure," he promised, shifting a little, putting himself into position for what came next, she realized.

Oh, God…

"There's a first time for everything," he said. "You know that, right?"

"Yes, but I've never been good at firsts."

"You'll be good at this," he said with such certainty that she had to believe.

He pulled off his jacket and rolled it up, sliding it behind her, making her as comfortable as possible, and she understood he did it so that she'd be better able to push.

She was going to have to actually push.

"It's going to be amazing," he told her, talking, keeping up the steady stream of words probably to take her mind off what was about to happen. "Beautiful."

"Beautiful," she repeated.

"That's right. Beautiful and life altering." He pulled off his T-shirt, which was eye-opening, and for a minute it pulled her out of her own world of pain because *wow*. He really had it going on, a tough, hard, sinewy built with more than few tattoos—

He spread the shirt beneath her hips. It was the only clean thing they had, relatively speaking, and this baby needed clean. She felt the panic bubble over. "Hunter—"

"Beautiful and life altering," he repeated. "You have to remember that. Be okay with it. Commit to it. Your baby deserves that."

That was true.

So absolutely true.

"Now." His eyes were dark, steadfast. "Let's do this. Let's have this baby. *Your* baby, Cece."

The baby she hadn't been sure she wanted until the day she'd felt something funny on her belly. Thinking a butterfly had landed on her or something, she'd looked down and seen nothing.

Because it had come from the inside. Her baby had kicked.

And from that day on, the baby had been hers, heart and soul.

She stared into Hunter's face, suddenly no longer overwhelmed with horror and embarrassment about the position she was in, or the position *he* was in. Instead, she felt his hope grow within her and take root. "Ready," she whispered.

His slow, warm smile was her reward. "Let's do this, then. Let's have this baby."

JASON MANEUVERED the raft down the flooded streets of Santa Rey, toward Lizzy's place. The going was tough, a virtual maze filled with death traps like garage doors, branches, lawn furniture and other debris moving along like bullets through the water.

He eyed the utter devastation all around them, the town so wrecked it'd lost its own sense of self, and felt the grimness settle in his gut.

He'd lost Matt on a day just like this.

And at the reminder, more than his gut hurt now. His damn soul hurt. How much suffering, how much destruction, he wondered, could a guy see and still remain attached? Emotionally involved?

Because he sure as hell hadn't been emotionally involved when he'd gotten here.

Or attached.

To anything.

He looked at Lizzy and amended the thought—*until her.* Too bad she'd made it clear she didn't plan on getting attached in return.

"I can't believe it," she murmured, looking shell-shocked as they floated along. "It's like a bad dream."

He didn't answer, because to him, it was a bad dream coming back to life, and then she took his hand. "Hey. You okay?"

He looked down at the hand that covered his, then lifted his head to look into her eyes, and caught what was happening behind her.

They were coming up on a big intersection, the two raging rivers colliding with an awe-inspiring amount of power. As he knew all too well, hell hath no fury like the power of rushing water, and this particular fury was incredible. Right where the two streets converged lay a whirlpool.

A swirling, massive whirlpool.

His heart sank, his gut clenched, and in the blink of an eye he was back inside that boat, watching helplessly as Matt lost his life. "Lizzy," he said hoarsely. "Get down—"

But it was too late. They flew into the vortex of the whirlpool and whipped around and flipped, and the next thing he knew the water was closing over his head. He pushed down, kicking to get under the water, not easy in a life vest, but he pushed hard to get to the place where he'd seen Lizzy go in.

He couldn't find her. Even when his lungs threatened to burst, he stayed down, searching. Finally his body forced him to the surface, where he whipped his head right and left, desperately looking for her as he tumbled over and over.

His blood was pounding in his ears, roaring as loud as the water shoving him along at breakneck speeds. The raft was right in front of him.

But no Lizzy.

"Lizzy!" Gulping in more air, he dunked again, and by some miracle, caught sight of her about ten

feet ahead of him, fighting like hell, just like she fought everything...life, love...and that's when he knew she was the one for him, the only one.

14

NEVER IN LIZZY'S LIFE had she experienced anything like the river that shoved and pulled and slammed where it pleased, which pissed her off, and she fought the current like hell.

It didn't help.

"Jason!" she yelled, or tried to, but the water swamped her mouth so she only got out the first syllable. She could see sky, and then the roof of a building she recognized, a light signal. Oh, hell, no way was she going to die like this. "Jason!"

But then she got rudely tumbled, and couldn't see anything but the frothy, churning water as it tossed her about as if she'd landed in the spin cycle of a heavy-duty washing machine. Fighting for air, she tried yelling for Jason again but her mouth kept filling up with water. Gross, icky water. And the oddest things kept going through her head.

She hadn't fed her goldfish that morning.

She hadn't yet held her new niece or nephew.

And she'd never let herself say *I love you* to a man. She'd never wanted to, but now, while being unceremoniously tossed around without will or way, she realized how sad that was, that she'd never opened her heart, not even with the one person to tempt her to do so.

Jason.

God, she'd been an annoying pain in the ass. Damn, the water was cold. Something rushed by her and she reached out for it, but it slipped through her fingers. Dammit. "Jason!" she tried again, but the water carried her voice away, choking her.

She struggled wildly to stop her momentum, to stand up, *anything*, but she discovered something right then, something a little horrifying. She was good in an emergency, but only if it was someone *else's* emergency.

Then, through her battle with the water, she thought she heard her name.

Jason. He had to be close by, and she struggled anew, nearly getting upright in the churning, rushing flood, which was good, because her lungs couldn't take another second.

A powerful hand clamped over her wrist and tugged, and finally, she got her head above water. Gulping hungrily for air, she gasped and coughed as she opened her eyes. Jason had her in one hand and the raft in another. He was letting the current whip them along through the worst of the rushing water, past the entire intersection, where it slowed. There, he swam them to the side, pushing her and the raft ahead of him. The moment she grabbed on to a bus bench, the water swirling up to the seat, she dragged in more precious air, feeling nothing short of sheer awe at what had just happened.

"Two-two," Jason said, and pulled himself up beside her, breathing as raggedly as she.

With a half laugh, she turned to him, arms open, and he swam right into them. "It's okay," he murmured, stroking a hand down her back. "I've got you—"

"I know." She tipped her head up, a relieved, grateful smile on her lips, which abruptly faded at the look on his face. He was pale, his eyes dark and haunted. "Jase—"

"You're shaking," he said, and tightened his grip.

"No," she realized. "That's you."

"Oh. Yeah. Sorry." He simply tightened his grip and buried his face into the crook of her neck, the muscles in his arms banded around her quivering.

"Jason—"

"Give me a minute."

He hugged her, then ran his hands down her body, making sure she wasn't hurt, but she grabbed them, wrapped her fingers around his and pressed them to her chest. His eyes were stark and bleak and broke her heart. They were full with grief and memories and horror, and she knew he'd been transported back to when he'd lost Matt. "Jason, look at me. I'm okay."

"Yeah. I know." He nodded and tried to pull away, but she grabbed his face and put hers right in his. "Jase."

He nodded again, then shook his head and closed his eyes. "I thought— When I couldn't see you, for a minute I thought you—"

"I didn't." She wrapped her arms around him and hugged him in so tight she couldn't breathe. But that was okay, he wasn't breathing, either. He was holding his breath, gripping her hard, and she ran her hands up and down his back, trying to soothe, to bring him out of it. "I remembered something back there. I forgot to feed my goldfish yesterday."

He lifted his head, his eyes clearer now, possibly even shining with humor. "You're something, you know that?"

"So I've been told."

His eyes never left hers. "I meant it as a compliment."

Her entire heart softened. "Jase—"

"Yeah, I know. We have to go." He held the raft steady for her to get in.

She looked at it. That hadn't been what she'd been about to say, but because she wasn't exactly sure what she'd intended to come out of her mouth, and because Cece was still out there, she did the only thing she could—she got into the raft.

JASON KEPT CAREFUL control of their progress, not interested in another Mr. Toad's Wild Ride. Hell, no, not when his heart was threatening to burst right out of his chest. He was concentrating on speed and direction and the fact that Lizzy was shivering wildly, when his cell phone rang, startling the hell out of him.

"I thought it wasn't working," Lizzy said through her chattering teeth.

"Me, too. Hello?"

"Did you just go floating down Third?" Dustin asked incredulously.

"Yeah." Jason whipped around, left then right, searching for his brother. "Where the hell are you?"

"Pull over."

Jason worked the raft to the side. Lizzy helped, grabbing on to a stop sign to hold them just as another boat turned the corner.

It was search and rescue, used on the lakes in the hills by the sheriffs who patrolled the rural areas. In it were a handful of rescue personnel, including Dustin.

Who immediately hopped into the raft and, right there in front of everyone, hauled Jason in for a tight, hard hug. Jason closed his eyes and hugged him back.

"Damn," Dustin said, voice thick, pulling free only far enough to look into Jason's face. "You're a sight for sore eyes."

"You just saw me a month ago."

"Eight. Eight months ago. Asshole." Dustin looked him over as if he was a piece of fruit on an inspection table.

"What are you looking for?"

"New scars. Hey, Lizzy," he said, without taking his eyes off his brother. "He treating you right?"

When she didn't immediately answer, Jason turned his head and met her gaze, which was surprisingly bright.

"Yes," she whispered, sounding like her throat was tight. "He's treating me right."

For some stupid reason, Jason's throat tightened, too, and he couldn't speak.

"Where's Cece?" Dustin asked.

"We don't know yet." God. God, look at her. She had an entire world in her eyes. And he knew right then it was complete bullshit that she didn't want to see where this thing could go.

Dustin finally turned to look at Lizzy, then took a second look before pulling Jason close. "Already? You've been home one day and you already slept with her?"

"You did not read that off me."

Dustin shook his head in disgust, then moved closer to Lizzy to hug her, as well, whispering something in her ear that made her smile.

Dustin said something else, and she gave herself away by giving a quick glance in Jason's direction, one that had him rolling his eyes at Dustin's back.

Lizzy burrowed into Dustin as if they were long-lost lovers, and ridiculously, Jason felt the green-eyed monster bite him on the ass. When Dustin turned and met Jason's narrowed gaze, arching a superior brow as he held *his* woman in his arms, Jason showed Dustin his middle finger.

Dustin merely grinned.

Oblivious, Lizzy squeezed Dustin's hand. "You're sweet."

Sweet? His brother was sweet? What about *him?* He was the one who'd gotten out of bed and leaped into the storm to help her, the one who hadn't left her side for over twenty-four hours. Dammit, he was the sweet one!

Dustin gave Lizzy one last hug, and then a damn kiss on the cheek that was only a fraction from meeting her lips, sending Jason another look over his shoulder before getting back into his own boat. "Are you sure?" he said directly to Lizzy.

"Sure what?" Jason asked.

"I'm sure," Lizzy said, and blew Dustin a kiss.

"Sure what?"

Dustin looked at Jason, his expression softening. "Yeah, definitely a sight for sore eyes."

And then he was gone.

Jason turned to Lizzy, who avoided his gaze as they pushed off and once again began making their way toward her neighborhood.

The silence grew until Jason couldn't take it. Even knowing he sounded like an ass didn't keep the words in. "He's taken, you know. And I've only met her once, but I can tell you this much. Cristina doesn't share."

Lizzy looked over at him, her eyes going so glacial as to nearly freeze his balls off. "Are you insinuating that I'm interested in your brother? *Sexually?*"

He opened his mouth but she held up a finger. "No, seriously," she said. "Is that what you're suggesting? That I would be sexual with you, while *also* being sexual with him?"

Well, shit. "I didn't mean it like that."

"Yes, I believe you did."

"Okay, I didn't mean to hurt your feelings."

"How about pissing me off? Did you mean to do that? Because *that* you succeeded at." She snatched the single oar out of his hand and whirled away from him, using her obvious pent-up temper to steer.

He grimaced. "You need to keep the oar—"

She sent him a death glare and he raised his hands, letting her continue. Incorrectly. He tried not to wince when they spun in a circle, then nearly hit the top of a parking meter. "I didn't think you were doing my brother," he said to her stiff spine. "It was instinctive. You were plastered up all over him, and—" He broke it off when once again she whirled on him, watching warily how she gripped the oar as if just by being in her hands it was tempting her to clobber him. "Yeah, about that oar," he said. "You—"

She slammed it back into the water, and unfortunately right into a pole. Before he could react, she went flying in the water. He spared one blink of an eye to sigh and think *"shit!"* before he dove in after her.

She saved herself so that by the time he got to her, she didn't need him. But he still kept his hands on her, helping her into the boat.

"Thanks."

She said it so begrudgingly he had to let out a short laugh as he hoisted himself up to the edge of the raft and looked at her. "And you should know, I kiss better than Dustin."

She stared at him, then planted a hand in the middle of his chest and shoved, dunking him back into the water.

LIZZY LOVED HER neighborhood. It had gone south in the eighties, been revitalized in the nineties, and had stood still in time since, so the houses were far more affordable than on the other side of town.

The water level hadn't risen as high here, only a few feet. Most houses they passed hadn't flooded, thanks to their concrete footings and foundations.

But the devastation still shocked her. Trees down. Cars buried under them. Roofs destroyed. Yards gone.

And it was still raining.

"Are you hanging in okay?" he asked quietly.

She looked at him, then closed her eyes. "Don't be nice."

"Why not?"

"Because it'll confuse me."

He blinked, then shook his wet head. "Okay, you're going to have to explain that to me."

"I really want to stay mad at you. So if you don't mind, you need to go back to being an ass."

"And you'll go back to what?"

"Being Lizzy. A sister. A nurse. It's what I do, it's what makes me happy."

"And a soon-to-be doctor," he reminded her.

Right. How had she forgotten that? "Yes, but the point is the happy part."

"Everyone should do what makes them happy."

"Yes," she whispered, wondering why then she didn't feel that way.

They turned the corner to her street, where they were able to abandon the raft and wade the rest of the way in. They passed her neighbor's house; Mike's okay, not too badly damaged. Her house was the last on the street. She'd lost a tree in her front yard, which had missed her roof by inches, but at least she still had a roof. She stared at the place in relief. "I half expected it to be gone."

It was tiny inside, postage-stamp tiny, with the kitchen and living room all together, and two little bedrooms off a small hallway, with one bathroom between them, but it was hers. All hers, cozy and neat, just how she'd left it.

And empty. "She's not here."

Jason walked through, his big, wet body making the rooms appear even smaller. He stopped in front of her, running his hands up and down her arms, making her realize she was still shivering. "Which meant she really did get out. That's a good thing, Lizzy."

Nodding, she tried to turn away, but he held her. "About us."

"Jason—"

"You stayed in Santa Rey when you could have left and gotten the life you wanted for yourself. That's admirable."

"I stayed because my sister needed me. We've been over this. You'd have done the same."

"Maybe. My family means everything to me, so yeah, probably. But, Lizzy, if I've learned anything, it's that at some point, you have to think of yourself."

The words, softly spoken and utterly from the heart, further compromised her calm. "I think of myself plenty. Hello, medical school in the fall."

"Before that. In the here and now. What do you do for yourself that makes you happy?"

Kissing you... "Okay, so I've been busy. Look, you're one to talk. You don't do anything for yourself, either."

"I'm on leave. I plan on doing plenty for myself."

The look accompanying that sentence singed her nerve endings and had her nipples hardening. "I'm not having this conversation," she said.

"Just one more thing then."

"No."

He slid a hand up her back, gently curving his fingers around the nape of her neck to tilt her head to his. "I like that you were stubborn enough to make your love of medicine work for you, even when becoming a doctor didn't work out back then. Now make something else work for you, as well. Something *besides* work."

"And I suppose by something, you mean *you*."

A ghost of a smile curved his mouth. "Well, I am standing right here."

"And leaving, soon enough."

His eyes never left hers. "Yeah. But what if I wasn't?"

She stared at him, her heart kicking hard. "Then I am. Leaving. Besides, you're not looking for a relationship."

"I wasn't, no. Things change. Life's too short."

Her heart skipped an entire beat. "We'd drive each other insane within a few dates, Jason."

"Chicken."

Lizzy let out a breath and went into the bathroom. Locking the door, she thunked her head against it. Lord, was she out of her element when it came to him. Pushing away from the door, she turned on the shower. There was no hot water, but even a cold one had to help.

THE BATHROOM LOCK CLICKED loud into the silence, the message clear to Jason.

Do.

Not.

Disturb.

Got it. He collapsed in exhaustion on the couch and leaned his head back, letting his eyes close for a moment as he heard the shower go on in the bathroom.

Without electricity, that was going to be one hell

of a cold shower, but hey, if that's what she wanted to do rather than face him, fine. At least out here he could have some peace and quiet.

Hell.

He didn't want peace and quiet. He wanted to be in that shower with Lizzy.

Stripping her, soaping her, touching her. Tasting her.

He opened his eyes at the odd sound, an unmistakable click of steel, a sound that reminded him of—

"Don't move," a man said softly, moving around to the front of the couch, holding a gun pointed at Jason's chest. "Don't move and I'll let you live."

15

THE COLD SHOWER didn't help. Getting out, Lizzy wrapped herself in a towel, and then froze at the sound of voices out in the living room. Her heart surged in her chest and she lunged for the door, because the only person she could think of who'd come here was Cece.

Please, God, let it be Cece.

She ran into the living room, tucking her towel between her breasts, dripping water everywhere, and skidded to a shocked halt at the sight that greeted her.

Jason on the couch, his hands up behind his head, wrists in handcuffs, which were locked around the wood beam that the couch backed up to, the one that bisected her small living room.

More shocking—standing in front of him was Mike, her neighbor.

Holding a gun.

"Mike!" she cried in shock. "What are you doing?"

Mike was fiftysomething, tall, reed thin, and an ex-cop. He'd been shot while on duty last year and medically discharged. His head whipped toward Lizzy, his eyes widening at the sight of her standing there in nothing but a towel. "Lizzy." He gulped, then quickly looked away. "I caught this guy trying to loot you."

"I wasn't—" Jason broke off when Mike waved the gun at him.

"You shut up." Mike was a good guy who'd been through some bad stuff, including coming back after being evacuated during the big fires to find his house had been robbed.

"Jason isn't a looter, Mike, he's..." She broke off and looked at Jason.

At her hesitation, Jason slid his eyes in her direction and arched an eyebrow.

Considering that the guy had a gun on him, he should be terrified. But he looked more annoyed than afraid, especially at her pause. "A friend," she said, not looking at him again. "He's a friend."

Jason snorted.

Mike frowned and took another peek at Lizzy, specifically her tiny towel barely covering her wet body, and gulped again. "Are you sure?"

"Yes," she said firmly, ignoring Jason's sardonic gaze. "Very sure. Please put the gun down."

Mike lowered the gun and rubbed his jaw. "Sorry," he said to Jason. "But we've been robbed blind before." He turned back to Lizzy, still clearly willing to kick some ass. "I've been checking for Cece, but haven't seen her. The cell service was so spotty, I couldn't call you." He stuck the gun in the waistband of his jeans. "Sorry again," he said in Jason's direction, and moved to the door.

"Mike? The key?"

"Oh. Right." Mike shoved a hand into his pocket and fished out the cuff key, tossing it to her.

Lizzy shut the front door behind him, then leaned against it and looked at Jason.

Stretched out and cuffed, the muscles in his biceps and chest stood out in bold relief. His hands held on to the beam, wrists bound, and she had one clear thought.

Sweet mother of God.

He was still wet, still big and bad, and if she wasn't mistaken, also fairly pissed off.

And sexy. God, so sexy.

"You going to bring that key over here?" he asked silkily. "Or stare at me all day?"

Lizzy approached Jason wearing only the towel and a matching blush. "I'm sorry."

He lifted a shoulder and watched her, hoping her towel would do him a favor and slip. It was the least she could do. "I have no problem with the cuff. I just prefer to be the one doing the cuffing."

She blushed deeper. Her knees bumped his as she fumbled with the key while trying to keep her towel from falling off. "I'm so sorry. I'm trying to free you. Hold still."

"Back in high school you once told me to let someone else make the first move." He jerked his hands and the cuffs clinked noisily, reminding them both that he couldn't make any move at all. "Maybe this is one of those times."

She went still. "This woman already made her move. She told herself no more."

"Because you're afraid."

"No. Not afraid. *Wary.*"

His eyes softened. "I'd never hurt you, Lizzy."

"I know that."

"Do you?"

"Yes." She had to kneel on the couch to reach his hands. Plus, she had to lean over him. Two things that worked in his favor, especially considering that the towel—the only thing covering her—got caught beneath her knees and very nearly slipped.

Unfortunately, she stopped and tugged it back into place, securing it by once again tucking the ends between her breasts. She reached for the cuffs. "Are you all right?"

"I'm not shot," he said. "So, yeah."

"He wouldn't have shot you." She grimaced. "Probably. Look, I really am sorry. If I'd known what was happening, I'd have—"

"What? Come running out here completely naked?"

She dropped the key.

He looked at it on the floor, then into her face. She nibbled on her lip and went to shift off the couch to get it.

Then stopped.

"What, are you enjoying me helpless and at your mercy?"

He'd only been kidding, but then she murmured with some surprise, "A little bit, yeah. I think it's the power. It went straight to my head."

He looked into her eyes and saw it, along with something else—excitement. "Ah, Lizzy, don't you know? You've always held all the power. Here…" He spread his fingers, the biggest gesture he could make. "Do what I've never let anyone else do. Have your merry way with me."

"Are you telling me you've never let a woman have her merry way with you?"

"Never," he murmured. "Be kind."

She stared at him, her hair falling like a silk curtain to her shoulders, her breathing speeding up a little. His did, too, because though he'd never had a bondage fantasy, he was nothing if not flexible.

And then there was how he felt about this woman. How hard he'd fallen. How much she meant.

He'd do anything for her.

Including this.

She looked down at him, at the way his shirt was clinging to his torso, molding to his skin. Her mouth opened a little, as if she needed it that way just to breathe, and he went hard. He knew the exact moment that she knew it, too, because her eyes widened and her breathing quickened. "We're mad at each other."

"Apparently certain parts of my anatomy didn't get that memo."

"Huh." She moved, and he thought that's that, she's done, but it turned out she wasn't done, not by a long shot. Slowly, she slid her thigh over his, lowering her weight more fully over him as her eyes drifted closed.

His entire body reacted to the sight of her straddling him, her lips parting in a hungry sigh, her hands going to the back of the couch on either side of his head as she rocked her hips to his and pretty much sent his heart rate through the ceiling. "Lizzy," he managed, sounding low and husky even to his own ears. He reached for her, came up against the confines of the cuffs and swore roughly. "God. I want to touch you—"

She slid her hands to his face, tilted up his head and kissed him.

Deep.

Long.

Hard.

No, she wasn't finished, not by a long shot, and she made a soft sound deep in her throat as she turned more fully into the kiss, not holding back.

He opened his mouth wider, moaning when she slid her tongue deeper, her hands tightening on him. He wanted to tighten his hands on her, too, wanted to run them up the outside of her thighs and under that towel where he knew she was all soft, satiny smooth skin.

But he couldn't, and when she broke off the kiss,

he was slow to pull back from the only connection he could make, taking his time, breathing her in, letting his mouth rest on hers so he could absorb the soft tremors that shook her, shook him. "God, Lizzy."

Humming her agreement, she kissed his jaw, his ear, revealing to him what she'd so readily denied with those very lips only a little while earlier—that she wanted him, that she needed him, that she felt more for him than she'd intended to reveal.

"Jason?" she whispered, her mouth on his throat.

His eyes had drifted shut, his fingers flexing, itching to touch her. "Yeah?"

Lifting her head, she held his gaze. She rose up on her knees, then got to her feet and, still looking right at him, her hands went to the towel tucked between her breasts. "For over twenty-four hours, you've done everything in your power to be there for me. To keep me safe."

"You kept me safe, too."

"I'm trying to show my gratitude here."

"Sorry. Carry on—" He swallowed hard as she let the towel slip an inch.

Then she dropped it to the floor, and the only sound in the place was his breath catching audibly in the silence. God, she was so damn beautiful.

"Actually, I have a confession."

Somehow he managed to lift his gaze to hers.

"I'm not that grateful."

"No?"

"No." She climbed back into his lap, giving him a heart-stopping view when she spread her legs over his.

Completely naked against his completely clothed body, she sat on him, eyes closed, mouth open, head back, her sweet, soft skin flushed, her body clearly aroused, and he thought he'd never been so turned-on in his life.

"Uncuff me so I can help."

"In a minute." She ran her hands up his abs, her fingers cool and not quite steady as she lifted his shirt. "Is that okay?"

"That you take a minute? Take as many minutes as you want, just please, God, don't stop."

She laughed and shoved his shirt up farther, pressing her mouth to his chest. She kissed a pec, then ran her tongue over his nipple.

Unable to stay still, he rocked up, and she wriggled, better seating herself on him. Her nipples were hard and pouty, and when he fought the cuffs, once again trying to touch her, her belly quivered. Her thighs were still spread, still revealing the most gorgeous view, disclosing exactly how turned-on she was, having him sprawled out beneath her like he was.

She did like her control, his Lizzy, and knowing how hot she was only made him all the hotter, and he thrust up again, until she let out a soft whisper of pleasure as his jeans rubbed at her.

"More," she whispered, and dipped down, taking her mouth on a little tour over the middle of his rib cage, nibbling at his abs…and then her fingers went to the waistband of his jeans.

And he held his breath.

"Are you comfortable?" she asked softly.

"Are you kidding? I have the woman of my dreams naked on top of me, her fingers in my pants."

"Before last night, I hadn't done this in a long time." She popped open the buttons on his jeans. "I don't know why."

"Because you didn't have a pair of handcuffs—*God,*" he exploded on a rough breath when she freed him, wrapped her hands around him and stroked.

"I didn't mean the cuffs. That's completely new. I mean…the sex. I think it's because I forgot how to let someone in."

Over the expanse of his chest and stomach, her gaze eyes met his, hers more open and honest than he'd seen yet from her and he reached to touch her, *needing* to touch her, but once again was thwarted by the cuffs. "Let me loose, Lizzy," he said hoarsely. "I want to touch you."

"Ja—"

"You're still in the driver's seat," he promised as she rose up and leaned over him with the key. "It's all you. I just want to—" When his hands came free, he ran them down her back, and because she was still leaning over him, her breasts an inch from his face, he indulged himself there, too, drawing the hardened tip into his mouth to suck.

Her response was to melt against him with a soft moan, her hands going to the back of his head, her fingers sinking into his hair to hold him against her.

As if he was going anywhere. He licked, nibbled and sucked, while she held him in her hands and drove him out of his mind with her strokes. He cupped her sweet ass, shifting her a little closer so that she could—oh, God yeah—run the hottest, wettest part of her over the hottest, hardest part of him. "God, Liz—"

She tugged at his shirt and he obligingly lifted his arms. Before yesterday it'd been a long time for him too, *way* too long. She could have no idea how he was barely holding on to his control here, but before he could mention it, before he could change their positions and lay her back on the couch to cover her body with his, she'd lifted up on her knees and guided him home.

When she sank down on him, she gasped out in pleasure, a sound that co-mingled with his low, helpless groan. "Lizzy," he murmured, hands going to her hips. "Let me—"

She rocked her hips and he saw stars. He'd wanted this to last forever, but he didn't have forever, not with her silken wet heat clamped around him and her breath soughing in and out in his ear, not with her hips pumping restlessly, with an air of desperation, as if she needed him so badly she could hardly stand it. With his hand in her hair, holding her head for his kiss, he shifted her leg, opening her a little more for him, so that her body was completely flush to his now, and just like that, everything in his world began to come together.

Or explode.

Depending on how he looked at it. He pushed up into her, a long, hard slide of slick, heated flesh that had her crying out in shocked pleasure as her arms went around him tight, holding on as if for dear life. "Jason— God, Jason…"

Yeah, the way she panted his name just about did him in. He tried to hold back, tried to hold still and just let it ride over him, the feel of his own body sliding in and out of hers, her soft, sweet body plastered up against him, but then she tightened, shuddered and, with a small cry, burst. Unable to hold it together in the face of her gorgeousness as she fell apart for him, all over him, he followed her over.

For what might have been forever, they remained wrapped up like pretzels, breathing like lunatics. He let himself absorb it all, her soft breath in his ear, her hands clasping him close, the feel of her little aftertremors.

Finally she pushed off him and rolled over to flop on the couch at his side. "Not a bad way to go out."

He rolled to face her and pulled her in. "That wasn't our last time."

"Yes, it was."

"Lizzy," he said very gently. "It's not going away."

"What isn't?"

"Us. Even though you want it to."

She swallowed and closed her eyes. "Don't."

"Why?"

"Because you're in transition. It's a bad time for this."

"Really? That's all you've got?"

"Okay, then it's because I'm going to Los Angeles."

"Which, luckily, is still on Planet Earth. I even know how to get there, imagine that." He dipped his head close. "This thing isn't going to go away, just like my feelings for you aren't going to. And pretend otherwise all you want, I'm going to bet it's the same for you." Because he knew his words needed a moment to sink in, he got up and went into the kitchen for water.

LIZZY WATCHED his sexy butt go into her kitchen, watched him grab a glass and turn on the tap while her breath caught in her throat, threatening to choke her. Standing up, she went into her bedroom and grabbed her bathrobe, and on second thought, her spare one, as well, since Jason's clothes were damp. She put on one and entered the kitchen to find Jason finishing a glass of water.

In the buff.

He set down the glass and looked at her.

"I've thought about what you said," she told him. "And I think you're confusing love with…"

He stroked a finger down her jaw. "Love?"

She gulped. Yeah. That. The one emotion she'd

never been able to tame, control or make work for her without pain.

Him being gloriously naked didn't help. She tossed him the robe. He held up the pink silk and, with a small smile, slipped into it. He looked ridiculous.

And hot as hell.

"I'm not confused, Lizzy. In fact, I've never been more clear. This isn't lust."

"It's been twenty-four hours."

"It's been over ten years. And here's the thing I've known since high school, but never had the balls to follow up on—you're it for me."

"Oh my God."

"I want this to work."

"This?" She spread her hands. "This is merely adrenaline, and okay a lot of affection and heat, but that's all in-the-moment stuff. I'm going off to get the life that's always been within my grasp, and you…you don't even know for sure what you're doing."

"So what? I still haven't heard a reason for us to throw this away." He crossed his arms and waited. In pink silk.

She gulped, torn between hysterical laughter and a horrible vulnerability. "Okay, it's not you. It's me." She paused, then admitted the truth. "It's all me. I…I don't get love. I don't trust it. I don't want it."

"That's because love's always cost you." He stepped close, dipped down to meet her eyes. "It's always been a burden, holding you back. It doesn't have to be like that, Lizzy, not with us."

"Stop." Shakily, she lifted a hand to hold him off as she shook her head and backed up. "I can't take you seriously in that thing. I'm sorry."

"Fine." He dropped it, smiling as silkily as the material of the robe. "Better?"

Was he kidding? "Okay, listen. I know what you're saying. Hell, any shrink out there would have a field day with this, my textbook fear of commitment. I lost my parents young, had to raise my sister, always had to be in control and now I can't give that up to share my life, blah, blah, blah…" She let out a breath. "Listen, you said you're screwed up, but the truth is, *I'm* the screwed-up one. Let's just leave it at that, okay?"

"No." He shook his head. "No, not okay."

From somewhere in the depths of the bathroom where she'd left her clothes, her cell phone went off. Grateful for the interruption, she whirled toward it.

"Lizzy."

She kept going.

16

L IZZY RAN INTO the bathroom for her cell phone. "Please," she whispered as she yanked it out of her pocket. "Be Cece…"

But the incoming number was unfamiliar to her, and she sagged in disappointment. "Hello?"

"Lizzy?"

It *was* Cece. Her throat swelled. "Oh, thank God. Are you okay? *Where are you?*"

"Well, I was halfway between my place and yours, in a Hummer, but now—"

"Are you okay?"

"I am now. Lizzy, this phone's going to die. Can you come?"

"Yes, of course, I'll come help you."

"That's the thing. I don't need help, I managed. On my own. Well—" She laughed. "Not on my own, not at all. Hunter was there with me."

"Who? And where are you?"

"We're…Hunter, where are we again?" Cece's voice broke off and then there was some rustling.

"Cece?" Lizzy said. "Cece? Who's Hunter—"

"That would be me," said a deep, masculine voice in her ear. "We're at the San Luis Memorial."

And that was it, the cell died. "San Luis Memorial," she said to herself, whirling to get dressed only to plow into Jason. He tossed her clothes at her as he hopped into his jeans.

"Come on," he said, and grabbed her hand.

She spared the split second to stare at him in eternal gratitude. "Jason. You don't have to—"

He didn't even slow, just sent her an annoyed glance over his shoulder. "Really, Lizzy? You're going to dump me *and* argue with me?"

No. No, she wasn't. "She's with some guy."

"Okay."

"No, you don't understand. She gave up men. We both did."

"Beg to disagree on that one."

She sighed. "I had a momentary slip. You sneaked in past my defenses."

"Right back at ya, babe."

CECE LOOKED UP at Hunter as he replaced the hospital phone by her bed, then leaned in closer and stroked her hair from her face. "How are you feeling?"

He'd delivered her baby and then managed to wave down a boat floating past them, who'd transported them to a roadblock and emergency personnel. From there they'd gotten a ride to the hospital in

San Luis Obispo, since Santa Rey's had been so badly damaged they'd not been accepting patients.

How did she feel after all she'd been through? "Shockingly good." She looked down at the sweetest little baby girl she'd ever seen. The infant lay on her chest, looking up with bright blue eyes, mouth pursed seriously. The peach fuzz on her bald head softened the rather severe expression, and Cece fell madly in love with her all over again.

"She's beautiful," Hunter said.

"Yeah." She paused, then screwed up the courage to voice the thought foremost in her mind now that she could breathe. "I guess it's over now, right?"

"Which? The storm?" Hunter glanced out the window and shook his head. "Not quite yet, though the worst has passed, I think."

"Not that." She paused. "This."

He paused, too, and she figured he had no idea what the hell she was talking about.

Hell, she barely knew what she was talking about.

No, that was a lie, and she no longer lied, especially to herself. She knew exactly what she meant.

"Cece." His voice was achingly soft, achingly deep as he hunkered down to her eye level.

Oh, God. Here it came. Another rejection. She should be good at them by now, but she wasn't. "It's okay," she whispered. "I—"

"I don't want it to be over."

She closed her eyes, then opened them and saw his steady, patient gaze. "You don't?"

Slowly he shook his head, then bent to press a kiss to the baby's head, and then Cece's mouth. They'd been through so much that she felt as if she knew him better than she'd ever known anyone, so it was a bit shocking to realize that it was their first kiss.

It was perfect.

Cupping her face, he looked into her eyes for a long moment, then kissed her again, letting her feel and taste the truth.

Yeah. He was right. It wasn't over.

Not by a long shot.

JASON GOT THEM back to his Jeep in an hour which, considering the conditions, was nothing less than a small miracle.

They didn't speak, which was for the best. Lizzy could sense his frustration, his hurt, and it killed her that she'd caused it.

She hurt, too. It was the one thing she'd wanted to avoid, and yet here she was.

Sporting a damn cracked open heart.

The rain finally slowed to an immeasurable drizzle as they drove back the way they'd come to get to the highway. Lizzy couldn't take her horrified eyes off the destruction. Houses had taken on up to ten feet of water depending on where they were and how high the foundations were elevated. There were bricks knocked off retaining walls, fences down, roofs missing. Entire streets gone.

"I can't believe it."

Jason managed to get them heading north along the coast with no mishaps.

And no words.

"Jason?" She hesitated. "Are we still friends?"

He gave her an inscrutable glance. "Is that what you want?"

It was the *least* of what she wanted. "I understand if you don't," she said softly.

"Really?"

"Yes," she said slowly, thrown by his disturbingly polite voice. "I realize I've confused things, Jason. Muddled up the relationship."

"Which was…what, exactly?"

"Uh…"

At her inability to put it into words, he let out a breath, revealing more frustration and a measure of temper. She'd finally busted through his infinite patience, which was quite the feat.

"You don't want to answer?" he asked. "Or you don't have an answer?"

She squirmed. Okay, so this whole talking thing had been a bad idea. "Here's the exit," she said, gesturing to the first off-ramp for San Luis Obispo.

"Code for shut up, Jason." He got off the freeway and drove straight to the hospital's emergency room entrance. "Go ahead," he said wearily. "I'll find you."

"Jase—"

"Go."

Right. She ran out of the car and into the hospital, thinking about his words. *I'll find you.* She knew it would always be true. If she needed him, he'd find her. If she wanted him, he'd find her.

Bottom line—he was there for her, through thick and thin and storms and panic attacks. He was there for her for anything.

Who was there for him?

At the registration desk, she was directed to a room where she found her sister sitting up in the hospital bed, wearing a gown and a wrist bracelet signaling that she'd been admitted.

"Lizzy." Cece's eyes went bright with unshed tears.

Lizzy rushed forward, so full of anxiety and worry she could hardly breathe as she reached for her sister, hugging her. "You had the baby."

"Yes. I had her."

"Her?" Lizzy's heart leaped into her throat. "It's a her? Is she okay? Are you okay? Where is she?"

"Right here."

Lizzy turned toward the tall, built, biker guy.

Holding a baby.

He looked at Cece, who nodded, and then he held the baby out to Lizzy, who took the bundle from his warm, solid arms.

"Meet Hope," Cece said, her voice soft and thick.

Lizzy stared down at the sweetest, most serene little face, at the perfect bow lips and bright eyes. "Oh, Cece," she whispered, awed beyond words. "It's your mini-you."

"Told you," the man murmured to Cece, and then with an undeniable familiarity, stroked his hand down her arm.

Cece didn't sock him. She didn't shove him away. She didn't flinch.

Instead, she smiled with her entire heart in her eyes.

Lizzy stared at the admittedly amazing-looking biker. "I'm sorry, who are you again?"

"My angel," Cece said.

"You're not the doctor," Lizzy said.

"No," he agreed. "I'm Hunter Bryant."

Cece entwined her fingers in his and gave him a sweet smile that blew Lizzy away. "Hunter delivered Hope," Cece said.

In Lizzy's arms, Hope cooed, and Lizzy stared down at her, heart melting into a little puddle at her feet. "Hope," she whispered, smiling as the baby yawned and stretched.

"Seemed fitting," Cece said.

Hunter smiled down at the baby, then at Cece. "It sure did."

"Okay." Lizzy divided a look between them. "Okay, what exactly happened out there in that cursed storm?"

"It wasn't a cursed storm." Cece smiled up at Hunter. "It brought me a miracle. Two miracles."

Jason appeared in the doorway, looking rumpled, edgy and exhausted. And yet when he saw Lizzy, his mouth curved, the smile reaching those gray eyes, softening him.

And Lizzy's breath caught. Cece was right. It hadn't been a cursed storm, not for her, either. Not even close… "Jason, come look."

Pushing away from the door, he moved close, shoulder to shoulder with her as he looked down at Hope. "She's beautiful." He touched the baby's cheek, his face softening even more into a sweet smile. He looked up at Cece. "Just like mom."

Cece let out another smile, this one sleepy, and she leaned her head against Hunter's chest, further shocking Lizzy.

"It's okay, Liz," she murmured quietly. "He's one of the good guys you've been telling me is out there."

As the baby yawned and nodded off, Lizzy felt Jason looking down at her, and she met his gaze. He touched her cheek as gently as he'd touched the baby's, running his thumb over her skin, catching the single tear she hadn't realized she'd let fall. "Ah, Lizzy," he murmured so softly as to be almost inaudible. "It's okay. It's going to be okay."

A promise. And he hadn't failed her, not yet.

Nope, the only one who had failed here had been her.

17

THE NEXT DAY, Lizzy went into work. The electricity had been restored, but there'd been significant damage to the east wing of the E.R., plus they were inundated with patients. She'd been running for four straight hours with nothing more than a shot of caffeine in her system when she was paged to the front desk.

She went hustling down the hall. It couldn't be Cece. Her sister was at home, doing wonderfully, and so was Hope. Lizzy had spent a couple of hours, holding her niece, stunned by the love that bubbled in her heart from just looking at the baby.

Then she'd gone to work, for the first time in her life just a little bit jealous of her sister, who had not only gotten her life together but was moving it forward.

Progress.

She needed that, too. Yeah, she'd had the UCLA thing planned, but she knew the truth now—it was no longer what her heart wanted, and hadn't been for a long time. She'd turned down the scholarship this morning.

She'd find a new dream.

As she headed to the nurse's station, she saw

Cristina standing in front of the desk with a clip-board. She was in full firefighting gear and looked filthy. She'd probably just pulled someone out of a fire and was checking on them. Cristina's partner, Blake, was across the hall, downing from the water fountain. Lizzy waved a hello in his direction and went straight to Cristina. "You okay?"

"I am." Cristina accompanied this with an amused look. "You?"

"I'm fine."

"Good, because there's someone here to see you." She put her hands on Lizzy's shoulders and turned her forty-five degrees so that she could see the other side of the desk.

Where Jason stood.

Unlike how he'd been almost the entire time she'd spent with him, he was completely dry. The odd thought almost made her smile, but she didn't. Couldn't. Not when he was standing so close, watching her, his eyes unfathomable, his hands tucked into his pockets, a pensive look on his face that turned into a smile when he saw her.

Not his full-wattage smile, not his usual confident-in-his-skin smile, but one that said he wasn't entirely sure of his welcome.

"You two had quite a time out there, I hear," Cristina said quietly.

"Yeah." She couldn't take her eyes off Jason.

"Do yourself a favor, Lizzy, and keep him."

Lizzy huffed out a breath. "When I suggested that to you about Dustin last year, you nearly bit my head off."

"Yeah, well, I'm meaner than you." Cristina accompanied this with a little nudge.

But Lizzy didn't need a nudge.

She didn't let herself think, she just did what came naturally, and walked up to Jason.

His arms closed around her, warm and solid. "Hey," he murmured in her ear.

"Hey." God, he smelled good. She wanted to bury her face in his neck, but she was extremely aware that she stood in front of the nurse's station and there were curious eyes on them, so she pulled back, firmly putting her hands in her pockets to keep them off him.

She'd told him she didn't want to do this, which had just been a way to protect herself, and now seemed dumb.

So very dumb.

In any case, she truly was so happy to be able to lay her eyes on him she could barely keep her heart in her chest. "I'm happy to see you," she said. "But what are you doing here?"

"I came to ask you out on a date. I was thinking lunch."

She had to laugh. *"Food."*

"Of course," he said on a smile. "So…? Yes?"

She couldn't believe he was standing here, looking so good. "A date? Really?"

"A first date," he clarified. "And why not?"

"Well, because we've already been through so much for one thing. The crazy drive, the white water rafting, the Olympic swim, the…um…" She felt her face heat as she thought of the other activities.

Naked activities.

"We've done it all," she murmured, smiling at the wicked gleam in his eye. "A first date seems… superfluous."

"We could go straight to the important stuff, if you'd rather."

Lizzy was very aware of everyone's extreme interest in their conversation, and she pulled him aside a little bit. "What's possibly left?" she whispered.

"Plenty. The I-love-you stuff for one."

She went utterly still, except for her eyes, which she felt nearly bug out of her head as she completely forgot about their attentive audience, which had simply moved closer to hear better. "I— You—" She closed her mouth, but she couldn't breathe so she had to open it again. "What?"

He gave her a knowing look. "Want to go back to just having lunch?"

"No," Cristina said for her. "She doesn't."

Lizzy shot her a look over her shoulder, then turned back to Jason. "I'm sorry," she whispered. "I'm…dizzy."

"That's panic."

"I'm not panicked."

"Oh, you're panicked," he said. "You're panicked and braced for the I-love-you stuff."

"Oh my God." She put her hands to her temples. "Okay, I'm panicked." Even with the spots and her blurry vision, his grin came through loud and clear.

"Let me put you out of your misery, Lizzy. I love you."

"I thought we were just—" She held up a hand. "Okay, you know what? I need to sit down."

So she did. She sat right there in the hallway and leaned back against the wall, staring up at the man who'd turned her world upside down.

He crouched in front of her.

Above them, from the other side of the nurse's station, came a scrambling sound as her co-workers and Cristina hopped up on the desk for a better view.

"You don't know what you're doing, if you're leaving—"

"Speak up," Cristina demanded, curling a hand around her ear. "Trying to eavesdrop here."

"*My* life," Lizzy said to her and the others, all now in danger of falling off the desk.

"Hey, if you wanted privacy, you should have gone to lunch."

"I'm not leaving town," Jason said.

Her heart caught. "You're not?"

"I know you are, but I don't care. L.A. isn't that far and—"

"I'm not leaving, either." She lifted a shoulder. "I'm happy here."

His smile was warm and melting. "Happy is good." He took her hand. "You were the first person to ask me what I wanted. Hell, I hadn't even asked myself." He put her hand on his chest, and beneath his shirt she could feel the steady drum of his heart. "You make me think, Lizzy. You make me remember that I have wants and hopes and dreams for myself. I want to stay. I want to wear a tool belt and renovate houses with Dustin. I want to get a big, slobbery dog. I want a relationship that lasts longer than a couple of hours. I want a future, *here*. And I want all of that with you."

"Aww," came from her co-workers in a hushed whisper.

"Shh," Cristina said.

Lizzy didn't take her eyes off Jason. "I'm stubborn, you know. And used to being the one in control. And—"

"Psst."

Lizzy tilted her head up and met Cristina's gaze, who was shaking her head and miming the slicing of her throat with her finger. "Ix-nay on the listing of your own faults."

"I realize you have lots of faults," Jason said solemnly, his eyes shining, giving him away. "Many, many, *many* faults—" He broke off on a laugh when she smacked him. "Come on, Lizzy, surely you can come up with something positive."

She stared at him. "I do like big, slobbery dogs."

"Atta girl." His voice went thick with emotion, the same emotion washing over her face and making it all but impossible for her to breathe.

Oh, God. She was going to do this. "I know something else."

"What?"

"I want to keep you."

Now that smile curved his mouth. "Yeah?"

"Yeah."

"That's a good start." His arms banded around her and he buried his face in her hair. "A really good start."

She gave up being tough and threw her arms around him as he pulled her in tight.

"Say yes, Lizzy," he murmured.

"To lunch?"

He laughed. "Yes, to lunch. To all your lunches. To us."

She pulled back to see into his eyes. "But I haven't even said I love you yet."

"Don't you?"

She had to laugh, even as she felt her eyes sting. "I do. I love you, Jason Mauer, with everything I've got." She let out a breath and repeated his words back to him. "So be kind."

"Ah, Lizzy. Don't you know? I plan on being everything you ever dreamed of."

* * * * *

Celebrate Harlequin's 60th anniversary
with Harlequin® Superromance® and the
DIAMOND LEGACY miniseries!

Follow the stories of four cousins as they come
to terms with the complications of love
and what it means to be a family.
Discover with them the sixty-year-old secret
that rocks not one but two families in...
A DAUGHTER'S TRUST by Tara Taylor Quinn.

Available in September 2009
from Harlequin® Superromance®.

RICK'S APPOINTMENT with his attorney early Wednesday morning went only moderately better than his meeting with social services the day before. The prognosis wasn't great—but at least his attorney was going to file a motion for DNA testing. Just so Rick could petition to see the child…his sister's baby. The sister he didn't know he had until it was too late.

The rest of what his attorney said had been downhill from there.

Cell phone in hand before he'd even reached his Nitro, Rick punched in the speed-dial number he'd programmed the day before.

Maybe foster parent Sue Bookman hadn't received his message. Or had lost his number. Maybe she didn't want to talk to him. At this point he didn't much care what she wanted.

"Hello?" She answered before the first ring was complete. And sounded breathless.

Young and breathless.

"Ms. Bookman?"

"Yes. This is Rick Kraynick, right?"

"Yes, ma'am."

"I recognized your number on caller ID," she said, her voice uneven, as though she was still engaged in whatever physical activity had her so breathless to begin with. "I'm sorry I didn't get back to you. I've been a little…distracted."

The words came in more disjointed spurts. Was she jogging?

"No problem," he said, when, in fact, he'd spent the better part of the night before watching his phone. And fretting. "Did I get you at a bad time?"

"No worse than usual," she said, adding, "Better than some. So, how can I help?"

God, if only this could be so easy. He'd ask. She'd help. And life could go well. At least for one little person in his family.

It would be a first.

"Mr. Kraynick?"

"Yes. Sorry. I was…are you sure there isn't a better time to call?"

"I'm bouncing a baby, Mr. Kraynick. It's what I do."

"Is it Carrie?" he asked quickly, his pulse racing.

"How do you know Carrie?" She sounded defensive, which wouldn't do him any good.

"I'm her uncle," he explained, "her mother's—Christy's—older brother, and I know you have her."

"I can neither confirm nor deny your allegations, Mr. Kraynick. Please call social services." She rattled off the number.

"Wait!" he said, unable to hide his urgency. "Please," he said more calmly. "Just hear me out."

"How did you find me?"

"A friend of Christy's."

"I'm sorry I can't help you, Mr. Kraynick," she said softly. "This conversation is over."

"I grew up in foster care," he said, as though that gave him some special privilege. Some insider's edge.

"Then you know you shouldn't be calling me at all."

"Yes… But Carrie is my niece," he said. "I need to see her. To know that she's okay."

"You'll have to go through social services to arrange that."

"I'm sure you know it's not as easy as it sounds. I'm a single man with no real ties and I've no intention of petitioning for custody. They aren't real eager to give me the time of day. I never even knew Carrie's mother. For all intents and purposes, our mother didn't raise either one of us. All I have going for me is half a set of genes. My lawyer's on it, but it could be weeks—months—before this is sorted out. Carrie could be adopted by then. Which would be fine, great for her, but then I'd have lost my chance. I don't want to take her. I won't hurt her. I just have to see her."

"I'm sorry, Mr. Kraynick, but…"

* * * * *

*Find out if Rick Kraynick will ever
have a chance to meet his niece.
Look for A DAUGHTER'S TRUST
by Tara Taylor Quinn,
available in September 2009.*

We'll be spotlighting a different series
every month throughout 2009
to celebrate our 60th anniversary.

Look for Harlequin® Superromance®
in September!

*Celebrate with
The Diamond Legacy
miniseries!*

Follow the stories of four cousins as they come to terms
with the complications of love and what it means to
be a family. Discover with them the sixty-year-old secret
that rocks not one but two families.

A DAUGHTER'S TRUST by *Tara Taylor Quinn*
September

FOR THE LOVE OF FAMILY by *Kathleen O'Brien*
October

LIKE FATHER, LIKE SON by *Karina Bliss*
November

A MOTHER'S SECRET by *Janice Kay Johnson*
December

Available wherever books are sold.

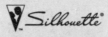

SPECIAL EDITION

FROM *NEW YORK TIMES* BESTSELLING AUTHOR

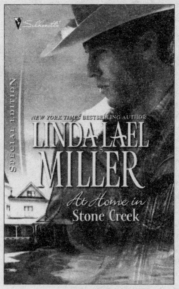

Ashley O'Ballivan had her heart broken by a man years
ago—and now he's mysteriously back. Jack McCall *isn't*
the person she thinks he is. For her sake, he must keep
his distance, but his feelings for her are powerful.
To protect her—from his enemies and himself—he
has to leave…vowing to fight his way home to
her and Stone Creek forever.

Available in November wherever books are sold.

Visit Silhouette Books at www.eHarlequin.com

SSE65487

You're invited to join our Tell Harlequin Reader Panel!

By joining our new reader panel you will:

- Receive Harlequin® books—they are FREE and yours to keep with no obligation to purchase anything!
- Participate in fun online surveys
- Exchange opinions and ideas with women just like you
- Have a say in our new book ideas and help us publish the best in women's fiction

In addition, you will have a chance to win great prizes and receive special gifts!
See Web site for details. Some conditions apply.
Space is limited.

To join, visit us at
www.TellHarlequin.com.

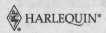

REQUEST YOUR FREE BOOKS!

2 FREE NOVELS
PLUS 2
FREE GIFTS!

HARLEQUIN®

Blaze

Red-hot reads!

HB09R3

Stay up-to-date on all your romance reading news!

The Harlequin Inside Romance newsletter is a **FREE** quarterly newsletter highlighting our upcoming series releases and promotions!

Go to
eHarlequin.com/InsideRomance
or e-mail us at
InsideRomance@Harlequin.com
to sign up to receive
your **FREE** newsletter today!

HARLEQUIN® *Blaze*™

COMING NEXT MONTH

Available August 25, 2009

#489 GETTING PHYSICAL Jade Lee

For American student/waitress Zoe Lewis, Tantric sex—sex as a spiritual experience—is a totally foreign concept. Strange, yet irresistible. Then she's partnered with Tantric master Stephen Chiu…and discovers just how far great sex can take a girl!

#490 MADE YOU LOOK Jamie Sobrato
Forbidden Fantasies

She spies with her little eye… From the privacy of her living room Arianna Day has a front-row seat for her neighbor Noah Quinn's sex forays. And she knows he's the perfect man to end her bout of celibacy. Now to come up with the right plan to make him look…

#491 TEXAS HEAT Debbi Rawlins
Encounters

Four college girlfriends arrive at the Sugarloaf ranch to celebrate an engagement announcement. With all the tasty cowboys around, each will have a reunion weekend she'll never forget!

#492 FEELS LIKE THE FIRST TIME Tawny Weber
Dressed to Thrill

Zoe Gaston hated high school. So the thought of going back for her reunion doesn't exactly thrill her. Little does she guess that there's a really hot guy who's been waiting ten long years to do just that!

#493 HER LAST LINE OF DEFENSE Marie Donovan
Uniformly Hot!

Instructing a debutante in survival training is not how Green Beret Luc Boudreau planned to spend his temporary leave. Problem is, he kind of likes this feisty fish out of water and it turns out the feeling's mutual. But will they find any common ground other than their shared bedroll…?

#494 ONE GOOD MAN Alison Kent
American Heroes: The Texas Rangers

Jamie Danby needs a hero—badly. As the only witness to a brutal shooting, she's been flying below the radar for years. Now her cover's blown and she needs a sexy Texas Ranger around 24/7 to make her feel safe. The best sex of her life is just a bonus!

HBCNMBPA0809